THE CHRISTMAS RESCUE

ELIZABETH KELLY

EK PUBLISHING INC.

Edited by:
L. Nunn Editing

Cover art by
The Final Wrap

THE CHRISTMAS RESCUE

By Elizabeth Kelly

Ivy West doesn't have time for love.

Especially while working full time as a vet tech and running her struggling animal rescue in her small Alberta town. She's content to secretly lust after her boss, Elias Hart, just like she's been doing for the last two years.

Except now he proposes a deal she can't pass up. Not when he's willing to write off the rescue's overwhelming debt to the clinic, if Ivy poses as his fiancée over the holidays.

Saying that Ivy was Elias' fiancée was a lie.

He knew it was wrong. But at the time, he would have told his sickly grandmother anything to make her feel better. Afterall, he never anticipated she'd pull through.

But she did.

And now he's expected to bring the sweet, sexy, untouchable Ivy home for the holidays.

With his and Ivy's deal made, their simmering attraction turns to flame that no extinguisher can douse. Until a mistake from Ivy's past surfaces.

Can Elias convince Ivy that they are meant to be? Or will Ivy's distrust tear them apart?

CHAPTER 1

"We have to call him, sweet girl."

"We do not have to call him, Nana," Ivy said.

"Listen to your grandmother," Bryce hollered from the far end of the porch. "We are in a crisis situation."

Ivy glared at her best friend. "Maybe if you'd stop being a giant chicken and get over here and help me, we could manage the crisis situation ourselves."

"Bock, bock," Bryce said before inching further away.

The unrelenting pressure around Ivy's waist and upper chest was starting to feel suffocating. She supposed that was the point. "Nana, let's try again. If you pull with both hands and I pull with my free hand, maybe we can -"

"It won't work, sweetheart," Nana said. "It's wrapped around you tighter than plastic wrap on a tuna sandwich. I had no idea snakes were that strong."

Ivy studied the snake coiled around her, from her hips to her shoulders. It was at least eight feet long and its scales glimmered in the porch light as its head weaved back and forth just above her right shoulder.

Its tongue flicked out, and Bryce made a sound of disgust. "Oh God, I can see its tongue."

"It's smelling the air," Nana informed her.

"How do you know that?" Bryce said.

"I just googled it." Nana held up her phone. "This snake looks like a common boa constrictor. Oh my goodness! They can grow up to ten feet long." She eyed the snake wrapped around Ivy. "I think this one must be fully grown."

She read her phone screen again. "Good news, dear. They're non-venomous."

"That's great, Nana." Ivy struggled to free herself with her one free hand again. At the touch of her hand around its body, the snake squeezed tighter, and she muttered a curse. "I think my ribs are cracking."

"Wait a minute, there's a note." Nana was now peering into the cardboard box still sitting on the porch. "It's a boy! His name is Jake!"

"Mazel tov," Ivy said, then winced again when the snake coiled tighter.

"Jake the snake?" Bryce said. "Lame."

"I think it's cute," Nana said.

"What else does the note say?" Ivy's bare legs and arms were covered in goosebumps, and her feet had gone numb about five minutes ago despite her slippers. Winter in Alberta was nothing to screw around with, and she cursed herself again for coming out onto the porch without her robe. Her beautiful, hairy, warm robe.

"Just that his name is Jake and he needs a home." Nana dropped the paper back into the box.

"We're a rescue for dogs and cats, not reptiles," Bryce said. "Do people not read the website? Also, what kind of person leaves a defenseless animal in a box on a porch on one of the coldest nights of the year?"

"Dearest, we have to call him. Your lips are turning blue," Nana said.

"From lack of oxygen or the cold?" Bryce asked. She was wearing her winter jacket over her pajamas, and she stuck her hands into the fur-lined pockets as Ivy watched with envy.

"Probably a little bit of both. Maybe we could ask Toby to come by," Ivy said.

Nana glanced down the dark road in the direction of their nearest neighbour's house before shaking her head. "It's after midnight, and you know Toby goes to bed by ten-thirty. Besides, Toby could be afraid of snakes just like Bryce."

"I'm not afraid, I'm *cautious*," Bryce said.

"Bock, bock," Ivy said.

"We know Elias isn't afraid of snakes," Nana said. "Didn't you say you have a couple of clients with pet snakes at the clinic?"

"Yes, but those are corn snakes," Ivy said. "They're little. He could be afraid of the big ones."

Nana just stared at her, and Ivy slumped in defeat as the snake bumped its head against hers before its tongue flicked out and touched the messy bun on the top of her head.

"Oh God, I'm gonna puke," Bryce said. "It's licking you."

The snake tightened again around her ribs, and Ivy winced. "Fine. Call him."

A PHONE CALL IN THE MIDDLE OF THE NIGHT WASN'T unexpected. As the only vet clinic in West Rilon, the small Alberta town Elias Hart had called home for the last two years, he often got phone calls in the middle of the night.

Nor was it all that unexpected that it was Lucinda West,

co-founder of Fuzzy Tails Rescue. West Rilon vet clinic had partnered with Fuzzy Tails Rescue long before he bought the clinic. There was always a rescue animal or two being treated at the clinic.

What *was* unexpected was Lucinda's assertion that her granddaughter, Ivy, was in grave danger of being squeezed to death by a snake.

"A snake?" Elias swung his legs out of the bed and scrubbed a hand through his hair. "What kind of snake?"

"A common boa, I think," Lucinda said. "He was dropped off in a box on our porch, and the minute Ivy picked him up, he coiled tight around her. He's just so strong, and we can't get him to unwrap from around poor Ivy's body. I know it's late, but could you be a dear and pop by?"

"I'll be right there." He tossed his cell phone on the bed and scratched at the scruff on his jaw before picking up his phone again. He called the number, tapping his fingers impatiently on his thigh as he waited for Alex to pick up.

Alex answered on the fourth ring, his voice scratchy and thick with sleep. "Dude. Do you know what time it is?"

"Hey, I need your help."

"It's sleeping time, asshole. Sleeping time."

"Alex," Elias said impatiently, "I need your help with a snake."

"Snake? What kind of snake?"

Elias could almost hear Alex's brain cells firing to life. "A common boa, I think. You still have that empty enclosure in your basement?"

"Yeah. The guy who was gonna give me his python changed his mind. You at the clinic? I can be there in ten."

"No, I'm headed over to Lucinda West's place. The snake was left in a box on her front porch."

"Shit. With the weather this cold, we'll be lucky if it isn't dead."

"It's not dead," Elias said. "It's apparently wrapped around Ivy, and she can't get it off of her."

Alex snorted with laughter. "Probably because she only weighs ninety pounds."

"She weighs more than that," Elias said. "Look, Ivy might be small, but she's strong. I've seen her lift dogs that weigh as much as she does onto the X-ray table. The snake's gotta be pretty big."

"They can get up to ten feet," Alex said. "Okay, you headed over there now?"

"Yeah. Can you meet me there?"

"Will do."

"Thanks, man." He left his phone on the bed and walked into the washroom, staring at his face in the mirror.

He wasn't sleeping when Lucinda called. How could he sleep when his life was about to implode in less than a week? His skin prickled, and the nausea that never really went away became a little stronger.

Shit. Why had he lied to his family? Did he really think that it wouldn't turn around and bite him on the ass? The lying had come from a good place, but it didn't negate the fact that his family thought he was engaged and expected to meet his non-existent fiancée in less than a damn week.

Not exactly non-existent.

He swallowed down the bile that was now rising in the back of his throat. His inner voice wasn't wrong. His family wasn't expecting to meet just any woman. They were expecting to meet – he swallowed more bile – Ivy West.

Co-founder of Fuzzy Tails Rescue, vet tech, and his damn employee.

CHAPTER 2

"That's a big snake." Elias studied the snake wrapped around Ivy's slender body.

"Isn't he magnificent?" Nana said.

"Real magnificent." Ivy stared at Elias. "A little help here?"

He moved past Nana, and the old woman reached up to give him a pat on the shoulder as he walked by. The cold weather and late hour hadn't deflated her spirits or her hair. She was as short and slender as her granddaughter, but he knew she was just as strong as Ivy. Years of wrangling big dogs had given her muscles that were more likely to be seen on men who roped cattle. He eyed Nana's shaved head and the short and spiky grey mohawk that ran down the center of her head before studying her arm.

"You get a new tattoo, Lucinda?"

"I did!" Nana's face lit up, and she shoved up the sleeve of her winter jacket so he could take a better look at the tattoo he'd caught peeking out of the sleeve. "Do you like it?"

"Is that a grilled cheese sandwich?" Elias stopped in his tracks and studied the tattoo in the light of the porch.

"Yep." Nana grinned proudly at him. "Bryce bet me a

hundred bucks and a month's worth of dog poop clean-up duty that I wouldn't get it tattooed on my arm."

"Who gets a grilled cheese sandwich tattoo?" Bryce called from the far end of the porch. "I thought winning the bet was a sure thing."

Nana laughed. "Never bet on an old woman who only has a few years left. We have zero fucks to give." She patted Elias's arm again. "Pardon my language, dearest."

"Not that I don't enjoy discussing the wisdom of a seventy-eight-year-old woman getting a grilled cheese sandwich tattoo, but do you think we could discuss it after you get the snake off of me?" Ivy said.

"Sorry, dear heart," Nana said. "Oh, who's this now?" She turned to study the car that was pulling into the driveway. Headlights splashed across the porch, and Elias cursed under his breath when he caught his first good look at Ivy. She was wearing light green shorts with a matching tank top and pink fuzzy slippers, and that was it. He could see the goosebumps on the pale skin of her thighs, and her entire body was trembling.

"That's my friend, Alex. He's here to help with the snake," he said before standing in front of Ivy. "Why are you dressed this way? It's the middle of winter."

"It's called pajamas." Ivy glared at him, her green eyes almost snapping sparks. She had one hand wrapped around the snake's body just below its head. The snake's head was resting against her skull just behind her ear. Its tongue flicked out repeatedly, brushing against her blonde hair. "I was in bed. If I had known that I would be stuck on the front porch for the last forty minutes being squeezed to death by a snake, I would have dressed appropriately for it."

He immediately suppressed the image of Ivy in her bed – would it be big enough for him to crawl in with her? – and reached for the upper body of the snake. "You should have thrown a jacket on before you came out on the porch."

She rolled her eyes. "Again, I did not picture this scenario when I went out to investigate the box."

He tugged on the snake. It didn't budge, and he pulled harder. He was a little surprised at how strong the snake was and, despite seeing how tough Ivy was at work every day, he could understand why neither she nor Nana could uncoil the reptile. Of course, it probably didn't help that the snake had Ivy's other arm pinned against her side.

He pulled again, putting some muscle behind it and, with reluctance, the snake uncoiled its upper body from Ivy. "You shouldn't be out in the middle of the night investigating a strange box on your porch, anyway."

"I thought it was a box of kittens." Ivy took a deep breath as, placing his other hand lower on the snake's body, Elias helped guide the snake into unwrapping.

"It's dangerous for you to go out this late at night," he said.

"Oh, please." She snorted in a way that shouldn't have been adorable but was. "Nothing bad ever happens in this town, you know that."

"Still dangerous." He didn't know why he felt the need to harp on her about this. Hell, he was pretty sure that she and her grandmother did way more dangerous things than investigating a box on their porch late at night, but he couldn't seem to let it go. "The next time this happens, call me and I'll come out and check the box."

She blinked at him, pulling her trapped arm free of the slowly uncoiling snake and flexing the hand a few times. "Are you kidding? Do you know how often we get boxes of puppies and kittens left on our porch?"

"You'd be here at least three times a week," Bryce called

from her spot on the porch. "Last night we found a large Tupperware container with a two-week-old kitten in it."

"Crap," Ivy said. "Speaking of, I should have fed Bender twenty minutes ago."

"You named the kitten Bender?" Elias said.

She just shrugged as Nana said, "Alex? Alex Berdmire? Is that you, dearest?"

"Hello, Mrs. West." Elias could hear Alex clomping up the porch. "Cold night, huh?"

"It certainly is," Nana said. "I haven't seen you since you were dating Alma's granddaughter. You two still an item?"

"No, ma'am. We broke up about four months ago."

"What a shame. A handsome boy like you should have a girl. Did you know Bryce is single?"

"Nana!" Bryce said.

A small grin crossed Ivy's face as Elias pulled the final few feet of snake from her body. The snake was already attempting to coil around him, and he turned and shoved it toward Alex before it could. "Here, Alex."

"Ooh, he's a beauty," Alex said. He set down the large plastic bin he was carrying and took the snake from Elias.

"His name is Jake," Nana said.

"Jake the snake?" Alex snorted. "Lame."

"That's what Bryce said," Nana replied. "Look how compatible you two are."

"Nana." Bryce's smile was more of a grimace, and Elias could see her face glowing in the light from the porch. "Stop playing matchmaker."

"I can't help it," Nana said. "I'm really good at it."

Alex cocked his hip at Elias. "Grab the pillowcase from my jacket pocket."

Elias pulled the pillowcase from Alex's pocket and held it open as Alex slid the snake inside.

"Will he fit in that?" Nana said doubtfully.

"Yep," Alex said as he carefully eased the rest of the snake into it and then twisted a knot in the top of the pillowcase. He took the pillowcase from Elias. "Mrs. West, can you open the lid of the bin?"

As Nana helped Alex put the snake into the bin, Elias turned back to Ivy. He studied the bluish tinge of her lips before his gaze dropped to her small chest.

Shit, she wasn't wearing a bra.

The clear outline of her nipples against her tank top was making the front of his pants tight. He was suddenly incredibly thankful he'd worn jeans instead of track pants. Ivy's arms clamped across her chest, and heat invaded his face when he glanced up. Her cheeks were red, and he fought the urge to cover his crotch when *her* gaze dipped to it.

"You're freezing," he said gruffly before shrugging out of his jacket and draping it over her bare shoulders. The cold air bit into his flesh, and he had no idea how Ivy had managed to stay outside this long in her thin pajamas.

"Thanks." She shoved her arms into the sleeves, the tips of her fingers barely peeked out from the ends.

"Why didn't you go inside with the snake?"

"We've got four dogs and six cats in there," Ivy said with an *isn't it obvious* look. "All of them rescues who, as far as I know, haven't been around a snake before. I wasn't taking the chance that they might try to kill it."

"Or have the snake kill one of the cats," Bryce said with a shudder.

"You could have put them in a different room," Elias said.

"I wasn't taking the chance," Ivy said stubbornly. "I'm responsible for those animals and I'm not doing anything that might put them in harm's way."

Before he could keep arguing, Ivy brushed past him. "Hey, Alex."

"Hey, Ives. How's things?" Alex held out his fist, and Ivy bumped it with her own.

"Good, thanks. You?"

Alex snapped the lid of the bin shut. The lid had about a dozen small holes, each the size of a quarter, punched in the top of it. "Can't complain. You can come closer, Bryce. The big bad snake is contained."

Bryce joined them, giving Alex a dirty look. "There's nothing wrong with having a healthy respect for animals who can murder you."

Alex laughed. "Common boas are one of the most docile breeds of snake around. They're rarely aggressive."

"Oh yeah? Because he just tried to squeeze Ivy to death," Bryce said.

"He was cold. He was wrapped around her and holding on so tightly because of her body warmth," Alex said.

"I didn't know you liked snakes," Nana said.

"All reptiles, actually," Alex said. "I've got a bearded dragon, a couple of leopard geckos, and an albino corn snake at home."

"What are you going to do with this one?" Ivy asked.

"I have an enclosure at home I can put him in," Alex said.

"Lovely. You're so sweet to come out here so late," Nana said. "Why don't you come in and have some hot chocolate before you head home?"

"Better not," Alex said. "This big guy needs a heat lamp and a place to hide. He's gonna be real stressed out right now."

"Join the club," Bryce said.

Alex grinned at her and picked up the bin. "See you at ceramics class, Brycie Boo."

She crinkled her nose at him. "Don't call me that."

Alex lifted the bin and nodded to Elias. "Later, man."

"Thanks, Alex. I owe you one."

"Yep." Alex tromped down the porch steps. The fresh snow that had fallen earlier in the evening squeaked beneath his boots, and they watched as he placed the bin in the back seat of his car and climbed behind the wheel. He waved before backing out of the driveway and heading down the road.

Ivy tapped him on the back, and Elias turned. She handed him his jacket. "Thank you for coming out here so late and helping us. I really appreciate it."

"You're welcome." He took his jacket, resisting the urge to press it to his nose and see if it smelled like Ivy.

"Okay, well, I have a kitten to feed. Thanks again. I'll see you tomorrow at the clinic." Ivy smiled awkwardly at him before walking into the house. Bryce followed her inside, leaving him alone with Lucinda.

"Can I entice you into a cup of hot chocolate?" she asked.

He hesitated. He needed to discuss the fake fiancée situation with Ivy at some point. Maybe now was the time to do it. He had, after all, just rescued her from a snake. Maybe it would make her more open to the idea of...

The idea of what? Spending Christmas at your parents' place? Pretending to be your fiancée so that your grandma and the rest of the family don't find out you lied? Why on earth would she do that? You and Ivy have a professional relationship, and that's it. Hell, I'm not even sure she likes you all that much.

He grimaced inwardly. His inner voice was right. Ivy had been cool and distant with him since the day they'd met. At first, he'd chalked it up to her being one of those employees who didn't like change – and there was no bigger change than a new vet buying out the clinic you worked for – but as the weeks and then months went by, he'd begun to wonder about that.

Out of all the vet techs, Ivy had been the most accepting of the changes he'd implemented, and she'd never once complained about new procedures or having to learn a whole new computer system.

She projected a *go with the flow* vibe that, frankly, he wished the other techs would emulate. He'd never mentioned this to her, but Ivy was his favourite tech to work with. She always kept her cool, whether it was when she was wrestling down a hundred-and-twenty-pound Burmese Mountain dog determined not to have a nail trim, donning leather gloves and handling a feral cat, or assisting him in a high-risk surgery. He could always count on Ivy to do her job well.

Honestly, he had no idea why Ivy didn't like him personally, nor did he know why it bothered him so much. He was her boss, and any relationship with her would be a huge mistake. If she quit the clinic, he'd be up the proverbial shit creek without a paddle.

Still, her obvious dislike for him made his upcoming confession to her even more damn awkward. And the hell of it was, he still had no idea why he'd blurted out her name to his grandma.

Maybe because you're stupidly attracted to her and have been for the last two years?

"Elias?" Nana was standing on the porch, patiently waiting for him to get his shit together.

He smiled apologetically. "Sorry, Lucinda. Yes, I'd love a cup of hot chocolate. There's something I needed to speak with Ivy about as well."

"Well, come on in. Mind the dogs," Nana said.

Taking a deep breath, he followed Nana into the house.

Here goes nothing.

CHAPTER 3

Her boss was at her house.

Her boss was at her house, and he'd just rescued her from a snake.

Her boss was at her house and – *oh God* – he'd seen her braless.

She grabbed at her small tits through the robe she'd yanked on the minute she stepped into the house. Her nipples were still hard as glass, but she wasn't sure if that was from the cold or the way Elias's face had changed when he'd looked at them.

He'd certainly never looked at her tits at the office.

Of course not, you idiot! Your boss is not attracted to you. He looked because your nipples were practically waving a sign in his face, and guys like tits, even teeny ones like yours. Get over yourself.

Behind her, Bender the kitten screeched even louder as he clawed angrily at the metal door of the nursery crate she'd set him up in.

"Okay, baby," she soothed as she took the homemade kitten formula out of the fridge. She heated it for a few seconds in the microwave, tested it with the tip of her finger, and syringed it into the small bottle. She poured some warm water into a plastic container, grabbed a couple of sheets of paper towel, and set both on the table.

One of their latest rescue dogs – a female forty-pound shepherd cross mixed with who knew what – weaved around her feet anxiously. Ivy couldn't remember what Bryce and Nana had named this one, but she wasn't sure if the late hour or her discombobulation at having her boss in her personal space was responsible for the memory loss.

The dog whined at her, her ears pricking forward when she heard Bryce coming in from the back yard with the other three dogs.

"You should have gone outside to pee," Ivy said to the dog as she grabbed the bottle from the counter and returned to the big wooden kitchen table and the screaming kitten. "You won't get another chance until daylight."

She opened the crate, grabbing the tiny kitten before it could worm its way out onto the table. She held it in one hand and pushed the bottle's rubber nipple against the kitten's mouth. He latched on immediately, drinking the warm formula with enthusiasm.

She sank into the chair, the shepherd mix rested her head on Ivy's knee, adding her hair to the already hair-covered fabric from the many – *many* – dogs who had come before it. It didn't seem to matter how many times Ivy washed the damn robe. It always had dog and cat hair on it.

Not that she cared all that much. It was comfortable and, more importantly, warm, and while it wasn't in any way a sexy robe, what did that matter? She didn't have anyone to look sexy for.

You could look sexy for Elias.

No, she couldn't. He wasn't interested in her. She knew

that, but no matter how many times she repeated it to herself, she couldn't shake her crush on her boss.

It's more than a crush, and you know it.

It wasn't, she told herself stubbornly. It was just a stupid crush she'd had for two years, and the fact that she suddenly didn't find any other guy attractive or interesting enough to date didn't mean anything. She didn't have time to date anyway. Between work and the rescue, her social life was nonexistent. After what happened with Ray, it was for the best.

She closed her eyes as the kitten sucked noisily at the bottle. Immediately, an image of Elias popped into her head. God, he really was handsome. His dark eyes and dark hair looked so good against his tanned skin, and had she ever seen someone with such perfectly straight teeth? He had to have had braces, right?

Despite her small stature, she liked a man with height, and at just over six feet, Elias fit the bill perfectly. More than one client had drooled over him in the clinic, and she couldn't blame them. His body was perfect, thanks to running two miles a day and exercising religiously. She'd seen him at the gym.

Not that *she'd* been at the gym. Forgetting that she couldn't afford the monthly fees, her dedication toward exercise was middling at best. She could thank her slender build to a great metabolism and spending most of her time chasing after rescue dogs.

So no, she hadn't actually been at the gym. But she had caught a glimpse of him working out on one of the machines as she'd been dragged past the giant windows that lined the front of the gym by a sixty-five-pound basset hound with a zest for life and a nose that just wouldn't quit.

It was only a brief look, but it was enough to fuel her

masturbation fantasies for a solid month afterward. At work, he wore either scrubs or a loose t-shirt and jeans. She knew he was in shape, knew that his body was hard and thick with muscle – she'd brushed by him enough times in their small surgery room to know that – but seeing him at the gym in a tight t-shirt and track pants that showed off his perfect ass? That was an unexpected and delightful gift. The way his biceps bulged, the way his shirt clung to his six pack… it wasn't right that one man could look so damn good. Could she be blamed for having an attraction to her boss?

No, she couldn't. And she wasn't the only one. All three of the other vet techs had a crush on him. Hell, even Joanna, their sixty-four-year-old receptionist, had a crush on Elias. Her notoriously crusty attitude disappeared the minute he smiled at her.

"Elias looked good tonight, huh?" Bryce had joined her in the kitchen. She sat down, smelling of cold air and snow, and the shepherd cross immediately tried to climb into her lap.

"Down, Zoe," Bryce said and gently pushed on the dog's chest. "Sit, girl."

The dog sat at Bryce's feet, her tail wagging madly, and Bryce patted her head. "Good job, girl."

"She's learning fast," Ivy said.

Bryce reached forward to run a finger down the kitten's back as it continued to eat. "Did you hear what I said about Elias?"

"Yes, and I'm ignoring it."

"Sweet of him to come out here and rescue you from the snake. Don't you think?"

"What I think is that I'm starting to regret admitting my crush on my boss to you," Ivy replied.

"Do you want cookies with your hot chocolate, Elias?" Her grandmother walked into the kitchen, followed by her boss, and Ivy stared at Bryce with panic in her eyes. Had he heard what she just said?

"Just the hot chocolate is fine. Thank you, Lucinda." Elias sat down across from Ivy but wouldn't meet her gaze.

Shit. He'd heard what she'd said.

She gave Bryce a *please kill me now* look. Bryce responded with a sympathetic smile and a *What are you gonna do* shrug.

Ivy took a glance at Elias. He was petting Zoe, who had wandered around the table to investigate his pant leg, and still not looking at Ivy. She turned back to Bryce and mouthed, "Do not leave me alone with him."

Her traitorous best friend gave her a thumbs up, then stood, faked a yawn, and said, "Well, it's late and I'm tired. Good night."

She was gonna murder Bryce the second Elias left the house.

"Good night, dearest. Do you have the other dogs in your room?" Nana asked.

"I do," Bryce said. "But Zoe's still not comfortable with them, so…"

"She can sleep with me," Ivy said.

"Okay, night, everyone. Elias, thanks again."

"Good night, Bryce," Elias said.

As Bryce left the kitchen, Nana set a mug of hot chocolate in front of him and one in front of Ivy. The kitten finished eating and, acutely aware of Elias watching her, Ivy dipped the paper towel in the warm water and wiped the kitten's private bits until he peed.

"Good baby," she murmured. "Good job, baby."

He screeched angrily, wiggling and squirming to get away from the warm water. She dried him with a soft towel and held him up against her neck in one hand. He immediately snuggled in, his cries of outrage turning to purrs as he awkwardly attempted to groom himself.

Nana added water to the kettle, set it on the stove, and turned the burner on before grabbing the hot water bottle from the kitten's crate. She emptied it and left it on the counter next to the stove. "Water's on for the hot water bottle, dear heart."

"Thank you, Nana," Ivy said.

"Well, I think I'll call it a night. These old bones of mine need some rest," Nana said. "Zoe, come with me, girl."

"She can sleep with me," Ivy said. "Your bed isn't big enough for you and her."

"Nonsense," Nana said. "There's plenty of room, and besides, you've only got a double as well, and you might have someone else in your bed with you tonight."

Nana squeezed Elias's shoulder as his mouth dropped open. Ivy wondered how wrong it was to hope that a sinkhole would open under the house and devour them all.

Her face bright red, she smiled stiffly at her grandmother and, through gritted teeth, said, "Good night, Nana."

"Night, dear girl." Her Nana's grin was positively diabolical.

Humming under her breath, she and the dog left the kitchen. Ivy sat in silence. What exactly did she say to her boss after her grandmother basically invited him to spend the night in her granddaughter's bed?

"Did your grandmother just suggest that you and I would be having sex tonight?" Elias finally said.

Her face still a flaming red and wishing that sinkhole would show up any time now, Ivy said, "She did. Welcome to my life."

There was silence for a few seconds, and then Elias said, "I didn't know Bryce was living here."

"She just moved in a few weeks ago." Ivy was more grateful than she could say that he'd changed the subject. "It's a temporary thing."

"Oh." Elias sipped at his hot chocolate. The whistling kettle broke the awkward silence. She stood up and held out the kitten.

"Can you hold Bender for a few minutes?"

He took the kitten, and when he held the tiny baby to his face, Bender licked his chin. Ivy was certain that the exploding sound she heard was her ovaries. Afraid she might join the kitten in licking her boss, she busied herself with turning off the stove, putting the leftover milk back in the fridge and cleaning the bottle. She filled the hot water bottle with the boiling water and wrapped it in a towel.

She stared at her warm and fuzzy robe that screamed sensible cat lady rather than naughty seductress, tempted for a moment to run to her room and change into something sexier and not quite so... hairy.

Like you have any article of clothing that isn't covered in animal hair. Even if you did, why change? Face it, Ivy, even if Elias was interested in you – which he isn't – sleeping with him is the stupidest idea ever. You need your job, and you need his support with the rescue. You almost lost the rescue because you thought it was a good idea to sleep with Ray. Remember?

She remembered.

When she turned around, Elias had snagged her stethoscope from where she'd left it on the table and was listening to the kitten's heart and lungs. He set the stethoscope down and examined Bender's ears, mouth, and eyes before checking his tummy and backside.

"He looks pretty healthy. A little underweight, maybe," he said.

She put the hot water bottle in the kennel without replying.

"You didn't bring him to the clinic today."

"He seemed healthy, and our bill is high right now. Just trying to save some money. Of course, with how fragile they are at this age, I'll probably have to bring him in at some point."

She leaned against the counter and rubbed at her forehead. Just thinking about the money that they owed the vet made her head throb dully. Even with the generous discount Elias gave the rescue, they still owed nearly four thousand dollars to the clinic.

The rescue relied solely on public donations, and Christmas was always a particularly tight time. Donations dropped at Christmas, and that dry spell extended well into January and February. While Ivy understood why, it was always stressful trying to keep the rescue going during the holiday period.

To make matters worse, their fundraiser volunteer had stepped down from the position nearly three months ago due to personal reasons. They hadn't found a replacement, and the rescue was suffering for it. She and Bryce had tried to pick up the slack, but they both worked full-time, and their free hours were spent answering calls from the public, going on rescue missions for animals, and coordinating the foster parents and volunteers. Her Nana had tried to coordinate a few fundraisers, but her plate was full with the adoptions. In between caring for the dogs and cats they usually had at their place, she called references, did home checks, and completed most of the admin work for the rescue.

It was only going to get worse before it got better. Hating to do it, but left with no choice, they had closed their doors to new intakes almost three weeks ago. But closing to new intakes didn't always go according to plan. Bender the kitten was testimony to that.

"Ivy?"

She glanced at Elias. "Sorry, what were you saying?"

He looked a little green around the gills to her, and she took Bender from him. The kitten had fallen asleep, and she set him inside the nursery crate on top of the hot water bottle before draping a large towel over the crate.

She sat down as Elias stared at his hot chocolate. "You okay?" she asked.

"I wanted to talk to you about something incredibly awkward," Elias said.

Her stomach dropped to somewhere around her knees. Shit. He'd heard what she said about having a crush on him. Feeling a bit nauseated – if she lost her job, the rescue really was screwed – she said, "You didn't hear what you thought you heard."

He glanced up at her, confusion written across his face. "What?"

"When you came inside with Nana, what I said to Bryce wasn't… I mean, it was just like a private joke between Bryce and me and…"

"I didn't hear what you were talking about," Elias said.

She slumped back in the chair, relief making her giddy. "Oh, right. Okay. Never mind."

"What did you say to Bryce?" he asked.

"Nothing," she said. "It's not important. What did you want to talk to me about?"

He cracked his knuckles and then picked up her stethoscope again, turning and twisting it in his hands over and over. "I thought you said you had cats in the house."

"Four of them are mostly feral and hide when someone they don't know comes in the house. The other two are seniors and spend most of their time sleeping on my bed or Nana's bed."

"Oh, right. I think Lucinda has brought in a couple of the feral ones before."

"She has," Ivy said. "So, what is it you want to talk to me about?"

"Honestly, there is no great way to say this, so I'm just going to say it." He took a deep breath and stared at a spot somewhere over her left shoulder. "My grandmother and my parents think you're my fiancée and that you'll be joining me to spend Christmas at their home."

CHAPTER 4

"You told your family that I'm your fiancée?" Ivy sat back in her chair. She looked a little shell-shocked, but Elias considered her not running from the room to be a hopeful sign.

"Yes," he said.

"Why?"

He took another deep breath, knowing he was about to sound like a complete idiot, but there was no way around it. "Do you remember when I took that week off in July?"

"Yes."

"My grandfather died, and I went home for the funeral."

"I'm sorry," she said. She reached out like she was going to take his hand before thinking better of it and tucking both hands inside the hideously hairy robe she was wearing.

"Thank you. As you can imagine, my grandmother wasn't handling his death very well. In September, she had a heart attack."

"Which is why you were gone for that week in September," she said.

He nodded, and she leaned forward a little. "Why didn't you tell anyone at work what happened?"

"I'm a private person. Anyway, it was just me and NeeNee at the hospital one night, and -"

"NeeNee?" Ivy said.

"It's what I call her." He could feel the blush rising in his cheeks when Ivy grinned at him.

"That's adorable."

"It was just me and NeeNee at the hospital, and she wasn't doing well. The doctor had told my mom and dad to expect the worst, you know?"

"I'm so sorry." All traces of humour had disappeared from her face.

"I was holding NeeNee's hand, and she was in and out of consciousness. Around eleven that night, she looked at me and she," he cleared his throat, blinking back the moisture that was collecting in his eyes, "was more lucid than she had been all night. She started telling me how sad she was that I didn't have anyone, that she was going to die before seeing me with someone I loved, someone I would want to marry."

He made himself look into Ivy's gaze. "She was devastated, Ivy. The look in her eyes and the grief in her voice, it – it crushed me. She was dying, but she was upset and worried for me because that's just the person she is, you know? Always thinking of other people."

"She sounds lovely," Ivy said softly.

"I shouldn't have said what I said, I know that, but I wanted to make her happy. She's my grandmother, and I love her more than anything. I didn't want her to die thinking that I was alone. So, I told her that I had a girlfriend and that I'd just asked her to marry me."

He could feel sweat running down his back despite the

coolness of the kitchen. "When she asked me about my fiancée, I panicked and said your name."

"Why me?" she asked.

He studied the paint chipped along the baseboard. "It seemed easiest. I could tell her we met at work."

"Easiest, right," she said.

"I didn't think it would go any further. We thought," he cleared his throat again, "we thought that NeeNee wouldn't make it through the night. But she did. She started to improve, and four days later, they were sending her home."

"That's good," Ivy said. "I'm glad she recovered."

"I was, too. Until the day we got her home and she asked me in front of my parents when I was bringing you home to meet everyone."

Was that a smile trying to bust free on Ivy's face? God, he hoped so. If she were finding this funny, he might have a chance at convincing her to play along with his ruse.

"I was going to tell them the truth right then and there, but NeeNee started talking about how knowing that I was in love and getting married was what helped her to heal. She was still devastated over the loss of my grandpa, but she said that my upcoming marriage was keeping her alive."

"Wow," Ivy said.

"Yeah." He rubbed a hand over the back of his neck. "I couldn't tell her I lied after that. So, I kept it going. I told my parents that I was engaged to you and I hadn't told them because we weren't dating very long before we decided to get married, and I was worried that they would think we were moving too quickly."

"They believed that?" Ivy asked.

"My dad did. My mother… she's a little more skeptical." He stood and paced back and forth in the kitchen. "They've been asking to meet you since then, and I've been putting them off by telling them you were busy with the rescue and work. Two weeks ago, my mom texted and said she and my dad were coming to town specifically to meet you. I didn't know what to do, so I..."

"Let me guess. You panicked and told them I was coming with you at Christmas," Ivy said.

He leaned against the counter and crossed his arms over his chest. "Yeah. It bought me some more time."

There was silence, and he watched as a brown tabby peeked cautiously into the kitchen. It crept forward a couple of steps, caught sight of him, and froze. It studied him before hissing quietly and slinking back out of the room.

"So, now what?" Ivy stared at him expectantly.

"So, now I'm hoping that you'll come to my parents' house for Christmas and pretend to be my fiancée."

"You're kidding," Ivy said.

"I'm not."

"Look," Ivy toyed with the ragged end of her robe tie, "I get that you think your grandma is only alive because you're getting married, but I promise you that isn't true."

"You don't know that," he said.

"I do," she said. "Your NeeNee is not going to drop dead when you tell her you fibbed about being engaged."

"I can't take that chance," he said. "If you had seen how bad she looked lying in that hospital bed. We almost lost her that night, Ivy. If I tell her the truth, it'll devastate her and probably put her back in the hospital. I can't – I won't – be responsible for killing my grandmother."

"Elias," Ivy's look suggested she believed he needed serious psychological help, "you're not thinking clearly. I can't pretend to be your fiancée. I hardly know anything about you."

"It's only Tuesday. We won't leave until the day before

Christmas Eve. That's this Friday, which means we have a couple of days to give each other a crash course on our personal information."

"It won't work," Ivy said. "I'm a terrible liar, and I can't leave my grandmother alone at Christmas."

"She can come with us." Elias could hear the desperation in his voice. "It's only for a few days. We'll leave on Boxing Day."

"I'm a terrible liar," Ivy repeated. "Ask anyone."

"You'll be fine. I'll help you."

"How?" she said.

He clamped his hands down on the counter, the bright edge of panic eating at his stomach lining. "Ivy, I get that you don't like me, but I really need your help here."

"What do you mean, don't like you?" she asked.

He didn't reply, and she frowned at him. "I like you, Elias. You're a great boss."

Her coolness toward him would suggest otherwise, but he kept his mouth shut. He needed her help. Pissing her off wasn't the wisest idea.

"I like you, but I can't pretend to be your fiancée. That's just – it's kind of crazy. You get that right?"

"I do," he said.

She stared at the crate with the sleeping Bender, and he knew without a doubt that he wouldn't be able to convince her to help him. Struck with sudden inspiration, he said, "I'll write off the rescue's debt."

Her head shot up. "What?"

"I'll write off the rescue's debt if you help me. It's what… three grand right now?"

"Four," she said.

"I'll write it off. The rescue can have a clean start to the new year."

"I can't let you do that," she said. "It's a lot of money and -"

"I want to do it," he said.

"No, you want me to be your fake fiancée and you'll do whatever it takes to make it happen," she said.

He sighed and sat back in the chair. "Look, I know the rescue donations are down, Lucinda mentioned it the last time she was in the clinic. You guys are on the brink of shutting down, aren't you?"

She chewed on her bottom lip. "Maybe."

"If you don't have the bill to pay at the clinic, you'll be able to make it through the holiday season, right?"

"Yeah," she said.

He sat back and let her think it over, keeping his mouth shut even though he wanted to keep talking, to keep trying to convince her to help him.

Dick move dangling the rescue clinic bill over her head like that.

Yeah, it was, but he was desperate. He loved his NeeNee, and he'd do whatever it took to keep her with them.

She glanced up at him. "If I do this, I also want a new microwave for the breakroom at work."

He blinked at her, and she said, "The one we have is the same age as Nana. It barely works, and I'm pretty sure we're all getting radiation poisoning from it."

"Done," he said.

"And you have to let two of our feral rescue cats live at your place until we can find them a home."

"Done," he said.

She eyed him suspiciously. "Seriously."

"Yes, I love cats."

"Does Bella love cats?"

Bella was his one-year-old pit bull, discovered as a puppy in a ditch just outside of town. She was brought to the rescue, and when Ivy took the sweet and good-natured white puppy with the adorable black eye patch to Elias to treat for worms and malnutrition, it was love at first sight for him. He'd officially adopted her within a week.

"She's a pit bull. She loves everything," Elias said.

She laughed. "Fine. I'll do it. But you can't blame me when it all goes terribly wrong because I can't lie worth shit."

"It'll be fine," he said. Relief was coursing through him, and he couldn't stop the big, stupid grin from crossing his face. "Thank you, Ivy. You have no idea how much this means to me."

She nodded and then tried to suppress a yawn. Feeling guilty, he stood up. "Sorry, it's way too late for this conversation. I'll let you go to bed, and we can talk more about this tomorrow at work."

"Okay," she said.

She walked him to the door, and he hesitated in the doorway. "Thank you again, Ivy. I'm sorry to ask you to do this, but my NeeNee is special to me and I..."

A soft smile crossed her face, and something in his chest tightened as she said, "I get it. I do."

"I'll see you tomorrow," he said.

"Good night, Elias."

CHAPTER 5

"Thank you so much, Heidi. You're a lifesaver. Literally." Ivy handed the blonde-haired woman the crate. Bender the kitten stared at her from inside the crate, and Ivy grimaced. "Don't look at me like that, stinker. Heidi will take better care of you than I would."

Heidi laughed and took the bag of supplies that Ivy handed to her. "I'll do my best. When was the last time he ate?"

"Um, I fed him on my last break for the day, so about three hours ago. He'll be getting hungry soon."

"I'll feed him when I get home," Heidi said.

"Thank you again." Ivy squeezed Heidi's arm. "You're my favourite fosterer. Have I told you that lately?"

"I'm sure you say that to all the foster parents," Heidi said teasingly.

Ivy laughed. "Maybe? Dr. Hart took a quick look at him, and Bender seems healthy, but you know the drill. Text me or Nana if there are any problems."

"Will do," Heidi said cheerfully. She nodded in Joanna's direction. "Have a good one, Joanna."

The receptionist barely looked up as she grunted out a goodbye to Heidi. She was shutting down her computer and turning the phones to voicemail. "Clinic closed three minutes ago," she grumped as Heidi left the clinic.

"Sorry, Joanna," Ivy said. "Heidi couldn't get here to pick up Bender until now."

Joanna made a harrumph sound under her breath before gathering her coat and her purse. "Make sure you turn the alarm on when you leave. Last week, the alarm wasn't turned on when I came in."

"I'll make sure it's on. Good night, Joanna." Ivy locked the door behind Joanna before leaning against it. Her stomach was a bundle of nerves, and she rubbed at the unidentifiable stain on her scrubs before heading toward the back of the clinic. Elias had pulled her aside at lunch to ask if she was up for exchanging personal details tonight, and she'd agreed.

Something she was starting to regret. She'd be alone with Elias, and while she'd been alone with him before at the clinic, this felt different. She'd be hearing all sorts of personal stuff about him and revealing her own personal shit, and oh God – what if he thought it was weird that she slept with a fan on all year round, or that she put jam on her toast first and then the peanut butter, or..."

"Watch out!" Elias's shout made her break out into a run. She pushed through the swinging door that separated the rest of the clinic from the waiting area. Something orange and hairy caught her peripheral vision, and she turned toward it.

"Ivy, duck!" Elias shouted.

She ducked immediately, covering her head with her arms as the large orange cat standing on the counter that held their lab equipment, launched his hairy body at her. The cat sailed over her head and screamed in outrage as he landed on the slippery tile floor with a muffled thump. His tail whipping back and forth, he screamed out another growl before streaking off into the cat room and disappearing.

"Oh God, Dr. Hart, I'm so sorry!" Whitney, their latest hire, was standing horrified near one of the three examining tables, a towel clutched in her hands. "I don't – I mean, I thought I had a good grip on him."

"It's okay," Elias said. "I shouldn't have asked you to hold the cat."

"You're bleeding!" Whitney's voice went up an octave and her face lost a shade of colour. "Oh God, am I fired? I'm so fired, aren't I?"

"You're not fired," Elias said as Ivy joined them. "Why don't you head on home? I'll get Ivy to help me."

"Are you sure?" Whitney turned to Ivy. "The cat is that feral one that your grandma brought in earlier, and I thought I could hold him, but he was really strong and then he sprayed me, and I…"

She showed Ivy her shirt. The front of it was soaking wet, and Ivy could smell the distinct and unpleasant odour of cat urine. Her eyes watering, she took a step back from Whitney. "It's okay. The ferals aren't easy to handle. Go on home, and I'll help Dr. Hart."

"I'm so sorry," Whitney said again. "Really, Dr. Hart."

"It's fine. See you tomorrow," Elias said.

Ivy decided that Elias was a much nicer person than she was. If Ivy had been covered in that much cat pee and – she studied the front of Elias's t-shirt – blood, she wouldn't be nearly as hospitable.

Mumbling another apology, Whitney escaped through the swinging door. When she heard the front door shut and the lock turn, Ivy said, "So… how's it going?"

Elias grimaced and then winced as he plucked his t-shirt away from his chest. "Fantastic."

"You smell terrible," Ivy said.

"Yeah, thanks. Do you mind waiting while I have a quick shower?"

Ivy shook her head. She'd thought it was a little odd that one of the first changes to the clinic Elias had made was turning the storage area next to his office into a shower, but after a few months, it made sense.

Not only did Elias often come to work directly from the gym, but his dedication to the animals in his care meant he spent a lot of time at the clinic. The shower and the cot that were permanently set up in his office were must-haves for him.

"Why didn't you wait for me to help with the feral?" Ivy asked. She had the most experience of the techs in the clinic, especially when it came to handling the difficult cats, and more often than not, she was the one who helped Elias with them.

"Whitney assured me she was fine handling the feral cats," Elias said. "I believed her."

"Oof, for how long you've been a vet, that is a surprisingly rookie mistake," Ivy said. "The newbies are always trying to impress the boss."

Elias chuckled, and the low, weirdly intimate sound sent awareness skimming down Ivy's spine. "Yeah, well, I won't make the mistake again."

"Go and shower," Ivy took a step back as another wave of cat pee aroma washed over her, "I'll get the cat into a kennel and settled for the night, and you can look at him tomorrow. I'm fairly certain he's healthy enough for neutering, but it's probably best to have him checked out first. Sound good?"

"Sure, thanks. You still up for learning some personal

details tonight?" His tone was casual, but Ivy could see the tension in his broad and probably very kissable shoulders from across the room.

"Yes. Look, I agreed to do this and I'm not going to back out of it, okay? I promise."

The tension eased from his shoulders, and he nodded. "Yeah, okay. Thanks. What did Lucinda say?"

"I haven't told her yet. Go and shower. You're seriously stinkin' up the joint."

Elias trudged toward the shower, and Ivy walked into the cat room. The room was on the large side, with two rows of kennels on either side and a small counter on the wall below the window. There was a small space between the upper row of kennels and the ceiling where they stowed extra supplies. The large orange cat had obviously jumped from the counter to the top of the kennels and had wedged himself in between a box of syringes and a box of gauze.

He stared resentfully at Ivy as she entered the room, growling under his breath.

"Don't growl at me, mister," she said. "We saved your life. It's too cold for you to be outside tonight. You would have frozen to death."

The cat growled again, and she rolled her eyes before opening one of the lower kennels. They were bigger and would give the feral cat more room overnight. Keeping her eye on the hissing cat, she inched over to the upper kennel he had been in, reading the name tag attached to the front of the cage.

"Warren, huh? Makes sense. Nana had an uncle named Warren. She said he was an orange-haired pain in the ass," Ivy said to the cat.

By the time she'd used some wet food to tempt and coax Warren into the large kennel, nearly ten minutes had passed.

She leaned down and stared at the big orange cat through the bars. "See you tomorrow, Warren."

She turned off the lights and left the room, closing the door behind her. She walked past the examining tables and the dog room to the back of the clinic, where Elias's office and the shower were.

She studied the door of the former storage area, her palms suddenly sweaty. She rubbed them on the thighs of her scrubs as her inner voice said, *Go on, Ivy. Join him in the shower, and see if he needs you to wash his...back for him.*

A delicious throbbing started at her core, and she squeezed her thighs together in an effort to ease it. It only made it worse, and she groaned inwardly. What was she doing? Fantasizing about joining her boss in the shower was a very bad idea.

Yeah, but don't you think knowing his dick size is something a fiancée should know? You're doing it for research purposes, Ivy. Research purposes.

"Shut up," she mumbled to herself, "nothing sexual is gonna happen between us. This isn't that kind of favour."

How do you know? Maybe he's expecting you to do everything a fiancée does.

Pleasure speared through her lower belly, and her nipples hardened. Was Elias expecting her to sleep with him?

Probably.

Oh God. She had just promised him she wasn't going to back out, but what if he did assume they would be having sex?

Too late now. You promised you would help him. Besides, what's that old saying? In for a penny, in for a... good pounding.

Her inner voice was stupidly giddy.

"Ivy?" The office door opened, and Elias, wearing jeans and a fresh t-shirt, stared at her. "You okay?"

"What? Uh, yeah, no, I'm fine. Sorry, I wasn't trying to be a creeper or anything. I just – I mean, I got the cat settled and he's all good now, so, uh, yeah, okay."

She stared at his thick, dark hair. It was damp and curling up along the back of his neck. She was itching to smooth it down with her fingers, and she curled her hands into tight fists. What the hell was wrong with her?

"Are you sure?" Elias stepped a little closer.

Oh God, he smelled so good. She didn't know what kind of body wash he used, but it was working for him. She wanted to latch onto him and climb his large body like a tree.

"Ivy?"

Feeling panicked, she blurted, "Do you want to have sex with me?"

"Wait, what?" Elias took a big step back, his hands held up like she was about to arrest him.

Her face bright red, humiliation soaking into every bone in her body, Ivy said, "What I meant to say is that this fiancée thing is strictly for show, right? You're not expecting me to…"

Elias blinked at her before suddenly twitching in under-standing. "No, absolutely not, Ivy. I am not expecting you to have sex with me while pretending to be my fiancée."

He spoke slowly and clearly, like he thought she might be a complete idiot, and she could feel her cheeks flushing again. "I didn't think so, but I just wanted to check."

"No problem," he said. "But I want to be clear that this is strictly platonic."

The look on his face suggested that he'd rather eat rat poison than have sex with her.

"Yeah, you made that clear." Did she look as pouty as she sounded?

Feeling stupid but still weirdly disgruntled by his obvious

disinterest in her, she continued, "But your parents and grandma will probably find it odd when we give off a buddy friendship vibe, rather than a romantic vibe because we don't touch or, um, kiss."

He hesitated. "Would you be comfortable with some handholding and a bit of physical touching when we're around them? Maybe a quick kiss occasionally to really sell it?"

"Uh, sure, that makes sense."

Ivy wanted nothing more than to turn and flee. Had she basically just begged her boss to kiss her? What was happening? Had she completely lost her mind?

"Great. Thanks, Ivy." Elias snagged his cell phone from his pocket. He seemed determined to ignore the tension she'd caused. "Do you like pizza? I thought maybe I'd order us something to eat while we talked."

"Pizza would be good." She rubbed her palms against her scrubs again as Elias turned to walk back into his office.

"All right. Come on in my office and -"

"Your back!"

The back of Elias's t-shirt was spotted with blood. He looked over his shoulder at it before shrugging a little. "Yeah, the cat got me on the back and the chest."

She followed him into his office. "What? How?"

"My back was turned when Whitney lost her grip on the cat and it launched onto my back, scrambled over my shoulder and down my chest," he said.

He was scrolling through his phone. "I'll use Uber Eats to get our pizza delivered. Do you like mushrooms on your pizza?"

"Elias!" She plucked the phone from his hand and dropped it on the desk. "Your back is really bleeding. Let me look at it."

"It's fine. I scrubbed it in the shower with soap a few times."

"I'll be right back." Ivy left his office and went to the row of lockers along the back wall. She opened her locker, grabbed the container of salve, and returned to his office.

"What's that?" Elias pointed to the container.

"It's a salve that Bryce makes. It heals burns and cuts, and," she made a face, "cat scratches amazingly well. Take off your shirt and I'll apply some to your back."

"Not necessary, I'll just put some of the meds we have here on it later," Elias said briskly. "What kind of pizza do you want?"

She crossed her arms over her chest. "This salve is better. Trust me. Let me see your back, Elias."

"I've been scratched hundreds of times, Ivy, I don't -"

"Then you know just how dangerous cat scratches can be. You won't be able to put the salve on your back without help anyway. Take off your shirt and show me your back."

He stared at her, and she returned his stare unblinkingly. "I can do this all night, buddy."

With a loud sigh, he turned around and stripped off his t-shirt.

"Yikes," she said. Despite her years of working at the clinic and the rescue, she was still a little horrified by the sight of his back. "This is really bad, Elias."

He just shrugged again as she studied his back. "I'll be right back."

She left his office, mixed up a solution of betadine and water, and grabbed some gauze. He was standing in the same spot when she returned, and she dipped the gauze into the betadine solution before gently wiping at his back.

He winced and pulled away, and she tapped him on his lower back. "Hold still."

"Christ, that stings. What the hell is it?"

"Just betadine solution." She studied the long red scratches that criss-crossed his upper back. They were already slightly puffy, and she cleaned away the rest of the blood before reaching for the container of salve.

She scooped some ointment onto her fingers and rubbed it across the scratches, coating them with the pale yellow salve. Elias looked over his shoulder, his nose wrinkling. "It stinks."

"Yeah, I know. But it works really well." She rubbed more salve across the scratches, trying to ignore how warm his skin was. Lord, those shoulders of his were impossibly broad.

Speaking of shoulders, he had scratches across the top of them, and she rubbed some salve into them. "How's that?"

"Better, actually. It's not stinging as much."

"Yeah, Bryce's salve has been a lifesaver," Ivy said.

"Could I get some for my chest?" Elias asked.

"Sure, that's not a…"

Her voice died in her throat as Elias turned to face her. Her cheeks heated up as she stared at what was possibly the most magnificent chest she'd ever seen. The light layer of dark hair on his upper chest was perfect. The defined slabs of abdominal muscles were perfect. The narrow line of hair that arrowed down from his perfect belly button and disappeared into his jeans was… perfect.

She was itching to trace a finger down that perfect treasure trail, pop the button on his jeans, and find out for herself if her boss was a brief or boxers man. Would it be so bad if she looked? That was something a fiancée knew, right?

"Ivy?"

She tore her gaze from his chest – good gravy, even his

flat nipples were the perfect shape and size – and stared at the container in her hand.

"Sorry." Her voice was thick, and she could hear the need in it. Praying that her boss didn't realize just how turned on she was, she scooped out more salve and set the container and lid on the desk behind Elias. The scratches on his chest were shallower, and no blood oozed from them, but they looked puffy and sore as well.

Be cool, Ivy. Be cool.

Her fingers trembling, she reached to smooth the salve across the scratches that marred Elias's perfect chest. Elias took a step back, his butt hitting the edge of the desk. "I didn't mean that you had to put the salve on my chest. I can do it myself."

Shit.

Was it possible for someone to die of pure humiliation?

"Right," she rasped out. "Sorry, I didn't…"

She didn't have a clue what to say. As the silence stretched out, she reached to smear the salve back into the container.

"But, uh, if you're okay with putting it on my chest, that would be fine with me," Elias said.

Her fingers hovered over the container. She stared up at him, unable to read the expression on his face.

"I mean, you've already scooped the salve out, right?" Elias said.

"Right," she replied.

She sucked in a deep breath, stepped closer to Elias until she could feel the heat of his big body, and gently rubbed salve into the first scratch. His chest hair was rough under her fingertips, his skin hot and firm.

As she rubbed salve into the scratch on his right pec, her pinkie finger skimmed across his flat nipple. He made a low sound in the back of his throat, and her nipples hardened again. The sound he'd made almost sounded like lust.

Stop it, Ivy. Your boss is not attracted to you.

No, he wasn't. He'd been nothing but professional since the day she met him. And until last night, when he'd briefly checked out her tits, his gaze had never roamed past her face.

Oh yeah? Then why did he tell his family you were his fiancée?

Convenience. Remember?

Her inner voice didn't reply, and, ignoring her urge to lean forward and press her tits against his chest, she turned her attention to the deeper scratch closer to his collarbone. This one had a bit of dried blood on it, so she grabbed some gauze, dipped it in the betadine solution, and gently wiped away the dried blood and the fresh blood that oozed out.

He winced and sucked in a harsh breath. Without stopping to think about it, she bent her head and lightly blew across the scratch. He groaned, and goosebumps broke out across his flesh. She blew again, and his hands curled around her hips.

"Ivy," he rasped, "what are you doing?"

She lifted her head and studied his face. The lust in his gaze increased her own need, and when he leaned against the desk and tugged her in between his open legs, she went willingly.

"Sorry," she said.

He didn't respond. He was staring at her mouth, and when her lips parted, his hands tightened on her hips.

"I really want to kiss you, Ivy."

CHAPTER 6

In his entire life, had Elias ever been so hot – so *desperate* - for a woman?

Ivy stared up at him, her pupils blown wide and her body trembling lightly under his hands. He bent his head and then stopped, his mouth hovering just above hers.

Shit, what was he doing? Ivy was his employee and –

Rational thought disappeared immediately when Ivy stood on her tiptoes and pressed her lips against his. They were warm and soft – so damn soft – and at the light, almost tentative flick of her tongue across his bottom lip, he groaned and pulled her up against him.

Her soft breasts pressed against his chest, and he slid one hand up to cup the back of her head. He angled his mouth over hers and pressed his tongue against her lips, demanding entrance. She moaned into his mouth and parted her lips. He took a taste, his tongue sweeping past her teeth to touch her tongue delicately. She tasted like the mints they kept at reception for the clients, and he deepened the kiss. She returned his kiss eagerly, their tongues tasting and teasing.

Her soft hands rested on his lower back, her fingertips tracing small circles back and forth over his spine.

Unable to help himself, he moved his hand from her hip to her ass. He cupped one firm ass cheek, squeezing lightly as her body arched and her fingers dug into his back. He shifted her a little between his open legs and pressed his aching dick against her flat abdomen.

She gasped into his mouth, and he tugged her head back and trailed a path of kisses down her slender throat. He tasted the hollow of her throat and nuzzled her collarbone before lifting his head to suck on her earlobe.

"Elias," she moaned when he squeezed her ass again.

He traced the shell of her ear with his tongue, then kissed her again. The soft moans and cries she made sent pleasure straight to his dick, and he pressed it against her again, needing her to feel how much he wanted her.

Her hand wandered down to his ass, and he groaned and reached for the hem of her shirt. He started to pull it over her head and hesitated. Did she want this?

Ivy made a noise of impatience and stripped her scrub shirt over her head, dropping it on the floor. He stared at her perfect breasts in the pale green bra.

"Elias?" Her voice was soft and a little anxious.

He smiled at her. "Beautiful, Ivy. You're so beautiful."

"So are you."

They kissed again, and he trailed his fingers up each bump of her ribs and cupped her breast. Her nipple was hard against his palm, and he squeezed lightly before rubbing his thumb across her nipple. She cried out into his mouth, her back arching again. He groaned and slid his arms around her slender waist. He picked her up, groaning again when she wrapped her slender thighs around his hips and rubbed herself against his dick.

He forgot about how wrong it was to sleep with an employee. Forgot that until this moment, he'd believed that Ivy didn't even like him. The only thing he wanted was to bury himself deep in her warmth and finally ease the never-ending ache in his dick that had appeared the first day he'd met Ivy.

He carried her to the cot and, with a few embarrassingly graceless moves, lowered her onto it. He landed heavily on top of her, and she made a soft grunt.

He raised himself on his forearms. "Sorry."

"That's okay." She grinned up at him.

He returned her smile before bending his head and kissing her collarbone. She arched and he pressed soft kisses across her upper chest – it smelled strongly of the salve that she had rubbed into his chest – before kissing her nipple through her bra.

"Elias," she moaned. "Please."

He tugged on the material of her bra, pulling the cup down until her breast was bared to him. He studied her perfect pink nipple and then pressed a light kiss against it.

"Oh God!" Ivy's fingers slid into his hair and gripped tightly. When he didn't kiss her again, she tugged hard, guiding his mouth back to her nipple. "Elias!"

Smiling a little, he licked a path around her nipple and then swiped across it with his tongue before lightly blowing on it.

She cried out, her body arching beneath his. "Stop teasing."

His smile widened, and he thought about teasing her a little longer until she squeezed his hips with her thighs and rubbed her warm core against his throbbing dick.

"Fuck," he muttered before bending his head and sucking her nipple into his mouth.

Her hands tightened in his hair, and she rocked her lower body against his as he teased her nipple with his lips and tongue.

When he lifted his head, her face was flushed, and desire had blown her pupils large. She stared at him, her lips swollen from his kisses and her body still rocking against his.

"I want you," she whispered.

He kissed her. "I want you too."

"Good." She reached between them and fumbled for the buttons on his jeans as he nuzzled her neck. "Get naked."

"Whatever you say, Ivy," he said with a slight grin.

He was reaching for the drawstring on her scrub pants when they chirped. They both jerked, and her pants chirped and buzzed again.

"Shit," she said and snagged her phone out of the pocket of her pants. "It's Nana. I have to take this."

He pushed his body off of hers and stood, turning away and adjusting himself through his jeans as Ivy said, "Nana? What's wrong? What? No, I'm fine. I was just, um, working a little late. Sorry, I should have texted you."

He turned around. Ivy was standing next to the cot, her bra covering her delectable breasts again. When she caught his eye, she crossed one arm over her breasts. He sighed, reaching for her top to hand it to her, then grabbed his shirt and pulled it over his head.

"Yeah, I'm just leaving now. See you soon," Ivy said.

He gave her a few seconds to put her shirt on before turning around again. Ivy shoved her phone into her pocket and smoothed her hair, then stared at the wall. "Um... so that just happened."

"I'm sorry," he said. "I shouldn't have -"

"No, it's on me. I kissed you first."

He scowled. "It isn't *on* you, Ivy. I wanted to kiss you."

"Right," she said.

The look on her face made him feel terrible, and he shoved his hands into his pockets to stop himself from reaching for her. It was obvious that she regretted what had just happened, and he felt horrible about it.

"I really am sorry," he said.

"Please stop apologizing," she said. "It's kind of making me feel worse."

"I'm sor -" He grimaced and ran a hand through his hair. "I mean, are you okay?"

"Fine. Do you mind if we, uh, talk about personal stuff tomorrow night, though? I forgot to tell Nana that I would be late, and she and Bryce are waiting on me for dinner."

"That's no problem," he said.

"Okay, good." She inched toward the door of his office. "I'm gonna go now. See you tomorrow."

"See you tomorrow." He watched as she practically sprinted out of his office.

"DOES HE HAVE A BIG DICK?"

"Bryce!" Ivy glanced at the open door of her bedroom. "Seriously?"

Bryce grinned before leaning against the headboard. "Listen, you tell me you almost had sex with your boss, and I'm gonna ask about dick size. You can't be surprised by that."

"I didn't see his dick," Ivy said in a low voice. "It didn't go that far."

"But it would have if Nana hadn't called you." Bryce petted Zoe's head. The shepherd cross rolled onto her back, staring adoringly at her. Bryce, her dark hair in a messy bun on top of her head and her body clad in flannel pajamas, rubbed the dog's belly.

"Yeah." Ivy sighed and pulled the quilt up. She tucked her robe tighter around her. "God, it's cold tonight."

"Nana turned the heat down," Bryce said. "She's trying to save costs."

"Yeah, well, she's got three dogs sleeping on her bed," Ivy grumbled. "She's in no danger of freezing to death. The rest of us aren't so lucky."

"Maybe if you didn't sleep with a fan on in the middle of winter, you'd be warmer," Bryce said.

"Shut it," Ivy said without much heat behind the words. "You know I need the white noise."

"There's an app for that," Bryce said.

Ivy just rolled her eyes. Odie, a brown tabby who was a little less feral than the rest, was lying at the bottom of the bed and grooming one paw lazily. When Ivy shifted in the bed, he paused with his paw held in front of his face and stared disapprovingly at her.

"It is pretty cold, though. If she turns the heat down much lower, we'll all have to huddle in one bed to keep warm," Bryce said. "Of course, if you have the delectable Dr. Hart in your bed, it might get awkward."

"He's not going to be in my bed," Ivy said. "What happened tonight was a mistake. In fact, it was all your fault."

"My fault? How was it my fault?" Bryce said.

"It was your stupid salve that got me into this mess."

Bryce laughed. "Look, it's not my fault that you and Elias are using the salve as some kind of kinky aphrodisiac. It's intended for medical purposes only, you perverts."

Ivy groaned and huddled deeper into her robe. "Oh God, Bryce. What have I done?"

"Made out with a super hot guy who you've been in love with for, like, ever."

"I am not in love with him."

"Gonna heat the bed with the old pants on fire method, huh?" Bryce said.

"Oh my God, I hate you."

"Nope, you love me, and you know it. Look, I don't see what the issue is here. You're gonna be his fake fiancée, right? It'll make it more realistic if you know what each other's o-faces look like."

Ivy glanced at the open doorway again. "Before we started making out, he made it clear that it was a platonic thing, that I wasn't expected to do anything sexual with him. Then I basically forced him to let me touch his chest and kissed him."

"I doubt you forced him to do anything," Bryce said with a frown. "He isn't the type of guy who would kiss someone he didn't want to. Plus, he *told* you he wanted to kiss you."

When Ivy didn't reply, Bryce said, "It's no big deal, Ivy."

"It is. Forgetting that he's my boss and signs my damn paycheque, the rescue needs him. What if we start sleeping together and things go badly? If he stops giving the rescue our discount, we are screwed, Bryce."

"He won't do that."

Ivy reached out and ran her hand across Zoe's fuzzy ribcage. "He might. I already messed up once by sleeping with Ray. I can't put the rescue at risk again."

"Elias isn't like Ray," Bryce said.

"We don't know that," she said. "Ray was a great guy right up until I found him in bed with another woman."

Bryce sighed. "Ray was a very accomplished liar. He had all of us fooled, Ivy. But I know Elias isn't like him."

"I can't take that chance. I almost destroyed the rescue

once. I won't make that mistake again. Nana would hate me forever." Ivy slumped against the headboard, watching as Odie twisted around to clean his spine.

"Nana would never hate you," Bryce said. "She loves you more than anything, Ives."

"I still need to tell her that we're going up to Elias's parents' place for Christmas."

"No can do." Nana, her mohawk still spiky despite the lateness of the hour, strolled into the bedroom. "I'm volunteering at the homeless shelter on Christmas Day, remember?"

"Nana, were you eavesdropping?" Ivy said.

"Don't leave your bedroom door open if you don't want to be overheard, dearest. You know I can't resist a salacious story, even if I have to eavesdrop to hear it." Nana sat on the end of the bed, crossing her legs and patting her lap. "C'mere, Odie-kins."

Odie studied her silently for a few moments before creeping across the bed and climbing into her lap. Nana petted his head gently, then reached forward and stroked Zoe's side. She smiled when Zoe's tail thumped-thumped-thumped against the mattress. "So, was Elias a good kisser? You never did say."

"Oh my God! Nana!" Ivy glared at her. "We are not talking about what happened between Elias and me."

"All right," Nana said. "But, just to be clear – Bryce is right. I could never hate you, dear heart. And I am positively exuberant over the idea of you and Elias being engaged."

"It's not real," Ivy said. "Did you miss that part? It's all fake. I'm only doing this to help Elias out and because he's writing off the debt the rescue owes the clinic."

She paused. "Oh God, that makes me sound like such a whore."

"Stop it," Nana said. "Whores have sex, and from what I overheard, you didn't bang Elias." She made a face. "That was my fault. Sorry, dearest. I have the *worst* timing."

Her face flaming red, Ivy said, "It's fine, Nana. It was good that you, uh, interrupted us. Sleeping with my boss is a big mistake."

"Oh, please, you have to live a little. Is it a good idea that I'm sleeping with the Widow Smith? It absolutely isn't – the man is a stage five clinger - but he's also an incredibly generous lover, and he has one of those fancy cappuccino machines."

Ivy and Bryce's mouths dropped open.

"You're sleeping with the Widow Smith?" Ivy said.

"Isn't he like eighty-five years old?" Bryce said.

"Yes, and yes." Nana petted Odie's soft fur.

"How? When? Where?" Ivy said.

"Well, mostly I ride him - he has a bad hip. Every Wednesday and Friday night. Friday nights at his place and Wednesday nights here," Nana said.

"Here?" Ivy's jaw hit the mattress again. "What do you mean here?"

"*Today* is Wednesday." Bryce eyed the doorway like she thought the Widow Smith might come waltzing through it buck naked at any moment.

"How did I not know this?" Ivy said.

"Well, and don't take this the wrong way, dear heart, but sometimes you're a bit of a prude about sex. I don't want to scandalize you, so I sneak the Widow Smith in after you've gone to bed."

"You told me that you spend Friday nights at Mrs. Jorgen's because you're too tipsy after your bridge game to drive," Ivy said.

Nana grinned at her. "I did. I am excellent at bullshitting

when I want to be. Honestly, I didn't tell you mostly because of the Widow Smith. If I introduced you to him, he'd think we were a couple."

She smiled at Bryce. "The Widow Smith is a great guy, but I like my independence."

"You call him by his first name when you're alone, right, Nana?" Bryce said.

"Oh God no," Nana said. "His first name is Elmer, and there is just no way to make that name sexy sounding, even in the throes of an orgasm."

"I'm not listening... I'm not listening," Ivy clapped her hands over her ears. "Bryce, tell me when it's over."

Bryce ignored her, leaning forward to study Nana. "So, you call him the Widow Smith in bed?"

"Of course not. Usually just Smith," Nana said. "But this isn't about my sex life, this is about Ivy's – or rather her lack of it. I really think you shouldn't be so closed off to the idea of sleeping with Elias, dearest. I never even understood why you dated Ray. You've been in love with Elias practically since the day you met him, and I'm fairly certain he's in love with you."

Ivy blinked at her. "Elias isn't in love with me, Nana. He thought I didn't like him."

"Well, you do act awfully cool toward him," Nana said. "I mean, I get why, but it really isn't necessary. You're allowed to follow your heart."

"It is necessary. He's my boss, and we need him for the rescue. He's the only vet clinic in town. If he fires me, I won't find another job as a vet tech, and we'll lose the damn house. And without that discount, the rescue will go under."

Nana flicked her hand dismissively. "Elias would never fire you or stop working with the rescue even if you did break up with him. He's too good and kind-hearted to be that cruel. Besides, you act like your relationship won't last. Who says it wouldn't?"

"I can't take that chance," Ivy said. "Not after what happened with Ray."

Nana made a gagging noise. "I always secretly thought that Ray had the potential to be a dirtbag, and what he did to you proved it. And his father turned out to be a right pompous ass too. God, they acted like the rescue owed them everything just because they made a sizeable yearly donation."

"A yearly donation that kept us afloat for six months of the year," Ivy said. "You have to admit, since Ray and I broke up and his father stopped donating, it's been incredibly difficult for us."

Guilt swept through her, and she stared at the dog and cat on her bed. Because of her stupidity, they'd almost had to stop helping innocent animals like Zoe and Odie. Hell, even now, it wasn't a sure thing that the rescue would survive the following year. All because she couldn't keep her damn legs shut.

"That isn't your fault," Nana said firmly. "The fact that Ray's father stopped donating just because his son pouted and acted like a world-class shit goblin speaks volumes about his character, not yours."

Ivy rubbed at her forehead as Nana said, "I love that you're being so sweet and helping Elias out with his fake fiancée situation, but I really can't join you over the holidays. The homeless shelter will be in a real lurch if I back out of my volunteer commitment. Plus, someone needs to be here to hold down the fort with the rescue, so to speak."

"Bryce said she would cover for us while we're gone."

"It's too much for one person," Nana said.

"Nana, I can't leave you alone at Christmas," Ivy said.

"Nonsense, I won't be alone. I'll invite the Widow Smith to join me after I'm finished volunteering," Nana said. "He'll make me his famous roulade, and I'll bang his brains out. It'll be the perfect Christmas."

"Get it, girl." Bryce held out her fist, and Nana bumped it.

"Speaking of which." Nana glanced at the watch on her bony wrist before lifting Odie off her lap and placing him on the bed. "He'll be here in half an hour. Do me a favour and don't come out to meet him when I sneak him past your room, all right? I like our little routine the way it is."

"I'll stay where I am," Ivy said.

Nana turned to Bryce. "Dearest, now that you know, would you mind terribly taking the other three dogs to your room with you for the night? The Widow Smith finds it intrusive when the dogs line up at the side of the bed and watch. Why, he can barely keep his erection sometimes."

"Nana! I shouldn't be hearing about your sex life. Bryce, please, for the love of God, get her out of here," Ivy said.

Bryce laughed and slid off the bed. "C'mon, Nana, let's get the other dogs into my room. Night, Ivy."

"Night."

Nana leaned down and kissed Ivy's forehead. "Sweet girl, I love you. I know you're committed to the rescue, but don't let it destroy your chance at happiness. Elias is a wonderful man, and I think you should look at this fake fiancée thing as an opportunity to explore a relationship with him."

Ivy smiled weakly at her. "Good night, Nana. Have fun with the Widow Smith."

"Oh, I will." Nana winked at her and followed Bryce out of the bedroom, shutting the door behind them.

Ivy stared at Zoe, who wiggled around until she was

stretched out in the warm spot on the bed left by Bryce. "Zoe, if you think I should bang Elias, blink twice."

The dog stared at her before lifting her tail and farting.

"Ugh. Thanks a lot." Ivy slid down in the bed and pulled the quilt over her head.

CHAPTER 7

"Thank you for agreeing to meet with me again tonight," Elias said.

"Thank you for picking my favourite restaurant." Ivy was studying the menu and avoiding his gaze. She hadn't looked him in the eye all day.

He sighed and sipped at his water. "Ivy, about last night -"

"We agreed we weren't going to talk about it," she said.

"I know, but I think I need to apologize again. I shouldn't have made those types of advances toward you and -"

She finally looked at him. "I was the one who told you to get naked, remember?"

He remembered all right. Hadn't been able to stop remembering it for most of last night and today. Just thinking about it now was giving him a semi. He shifted forward on his chair, ignoring the pressure on his groin and incredibly thankful that the table hid his lap.

"I just don't want you thinking that I'm some kind of predator who preys on my employees."

Her mouth dropped open before she shook her head. "Are you kidding? Elias, I don't think that. I've *never* thought that.

No one does. Everyone at work thinks you're a fantastic boss, and you're always professional."

Some of the tension leaked out of his body as she said, "Look. I know I've been… weird today at work, but it's because I'm horribly embarrassed."

"Don't be," he said. "It's no big deal. Obviously, we're attracted to each other and sometimes stuff happens."

"Right," she said with a small grimace. "But losing my job because I slept with my boss is -"

"You wouldn't lose your job," he said quickly. "Not that we're going to sleep together because we're not. I'm your boss, you're my employee, and it's all kinds of inappropriate for me to sleep with you. But *if* we had slept together last night, I would never fire you over it. I promise, Ivy."

He could see some of *her* tension easing. "Okay, thank you for saying that."

"It's the truth," he said. "And I apologize again for my loss of control last night." He took a deep breath and decided to be completely honest. "I've been attracted to you for a very long time, and last night, I just…"

He didn't know how to finish the sentence, but Ivy nodded. "I get it. I thought you were hot the first day you walked into the clinic."

"You did a good job of hiding it," he said. "I was sure you didn't like me as a boss or as a person."

She flinched. "God, that's awful. I'm sorry. I didn't mean to come across that way."

"It's fine," he said. "We still make a pretty good team at the clinic."

She smiled at him, and his heart did this stupid thing where it skipped a beat or two. "We are a good team. I enjoy working with you, Elias."

"I like working with you," he said. "Very much. Don't tell

the other techs, but you're my go-to person for cat wrangling."

She laughed. "I think everyone at the clinic already knows that."

The server arrived and they placed their orders. Elias smiled at Ivy. "So, one last thing." He pulled out a small box and, with a quick look around, set it near her plate. "This is, uh, an engagement ring."

She stared at him. "Holy shit. Tell me you didn't buy a ring to sell this story, because we could tell them the ring was in for sizing or something."

He laughed. "The ring is actually my NeeNee's. It was the first engagement ring my grandfather gave her, and she passed it down to me before I left for vet school. Poppa had bought her another one that was bigger and more expensive for their twentieth anniversary, but she kept this original one. She wanted me to give it to my fiancée, and I didn't have the heart to tell her no."

He could feel his cheeks heating up. "The diamond is minuscule and I'm pretty sure my grandpa only paid about two hundred bucks for it, but NeeNee would be thrilled if you're wearing it or at the very least, tell her that I gave it to you and you love it, if it doesn't fit."

She opened the box and studied the silver ring with the tiny diamond embedded in a heart-shaped frame. "It's beautiful."

He shrugged. "It's small and maybe a little plain, but NeeNee said that Poppa saved up for over a year to buy it for her. She loved it and it means a lot to her."

Ivy carefully lifted it from the box and slipped it onto her left ring finger. A weird ripple of excitement went down his spine when he saw his grandmother's ring on her finger. "It looks like it fits," he said.

"It fits perfectly." She studied the ring. "Are you sure you want me to wear this, though? I mean, it's special to your grandma and to you, so maybe you want the first woman to wear it to be your actual fiancée?"

"I want you to wear it," he said. "It would mean a lot to me."

"And my NeeNee," he said hastily when she looked up at him.

"All right." She slipped off the ring and replaced it in the box, closing it carefully and tucking it into her purse. "I'll put it on tomorrow before we get to your parents' place."

"Thanks," he said. "So, I think I'm ready for my crash course on all things Ivy West. Hit me."

She toyed with the napkin before unwrapping it from the silverware and placing it on her lap. "Let's see. I'm twenty-eight, my birthday is August 27th, and my favourite colour is green. I'm an only child. My parents' names are Joyce and William. Mom was a stay-at-home mom, and my dad managed the Pick-n-Pull off Highway 62 for over thirty years. He retired four years ago, and they bought one of those big RVs and traveled across Canada for a year."

"That's cool," Elias said.

She nodded. "It'd been my dad's dream for years. Anyway, they saw all of Canada, and then they parked the RV permanently in Victoria. The warmer weather is better for Dad's arthritis."

"You must miss them," Elias said.

"I do. They usually drive or fly out once or twice a year to see us. I've been to Victoria a few times as well. It's so beautiful there."

"Have you considered moving there to be closer to them?" Elias asked. There was a weird tightness in his chest at the thought of Ivy leaving.

"No," Ivy said. "I love Alberta, and so does Nana. She would never leave, and I would never leave her. It's not just that either. We'd have to shut down the rescue, and it's not like our little town is bustling with animal rescue groups who could fill the void."

"That's true," he said. "Although I was talking to Alma Morin when she brought her ferret in the other day, and she's thinking about starting up a rescue."

"She is," Ivy said. "But it would be for small animals only. There's nothing in place for cats and dogs in West Rilon. It's why we started the rescue in the first place."

The food arrived, and they ate the first few bites before Elias said, "So, tell me some more about yourself."

She laughed. "Now I feel like I'm on a first date."

Elias glanced at the other people in the restaurant. "How fast do you think the rumour will spread that we're dating just because we're having dinner together at a restaurant?"

"In this town? They'll have us married and expecting our first kid by the end of the week," Ivy said.

Elias groaned. "Probably. God, I still haven't got used to the small-town gossip thing."

"You grew up in a small town, didn't you?" she asked.

"Yes, my parents have lived in Hillstone my entire life. But after I did my vet schooling in Saskatoon, I moved to Toronto, and I guess I became accustomed to the anonymous lifestyle in a big city."

"What made you decide to move here?" Ivy asked.

"A few reasons," he said. "It's closer to my parents, I wasn't a big fan of big city living, and I wanted my own clinic. Alex sent me a text one day telling me the clinic was for sale. I met with Dr. Sorenson, made her an offer, and she accepted."

"And now you're here," Ivy said softly.

"And now I'm here." He ate some more of his pasta as Ivy stared thoughtfully at him.

"So, you and Alex were friends before you moved here?"

"Yes. We grew up together in Hillstone. Alex moved here around the same time I moved to Toronto. But we've always kept in touch. He's a good guy."

"I don't know him very well," Ivy said. "Other than seeing him a couple of times at the clinic. Bryce started taking a pottery class over at the Rilon Centre, and I guess Alex goes to the same class."

"He's mentioned her a couple of times," Elias said.

"Does he like her?" Ivy paused with her fork in the air.

"Maybe? He hasn't really said either way," Elias replied. "Why? Does she like him?"

"She had a bad break-up a few months ago," Ivy said. "I don't think she's ready to start dating again yet. Anyway, this isn't supposed to be about Alex and Bryce. Tell me some more stuff about you."

"I feel like I haven't learned enough about you yet," he said with a small grin.

"Okay, um, let's see." She tapped her fork on the edge of her plate. "I love coffee – really love it – and am meh about tea. I'm allergic to curry and I hate apples."

"Seriously? I've never met someone who hates apples," he said.

"Well, now you have," she said primly.

He laughed. "Did you have some apple-related trauma as a child?"

"Nope. They're just gross. I hate the way they feel against your teeth when you bite into them." She shuddered. "Yuck."

"Hates apples. Got it," he said with another grin.

"There has to be a food you hate," she said.

"Sadly, no. My love of food is legendary back in Hillstone.

It's why I hit the gym every morning." He stared down at his nearly empty plate of pasta. "You're totally worth every bite, though."

There was a moment of silence, and when he looked up, Ivy said, "Should I leave you and the pasta alone together or…"

"We're good," he said. "As long as you understand that pasta is, and always will be, my first love."

"My fake fiancé has a weird pasta obsession. Noted." She made a check mark in the air with her finger. "Hit me with the next bit of Elias weirdness, I'm ready."

"That's probably the weirdest thing about me," he said with a laugh. "I'm thirty-two, my birthday is July 16th, I'm an only child as well, I drink tea *and* coffee, and I have no allergies. My mom is Barbara, my dad is Doug, and they own a dairy farm about twenty kilometers outside of Hillstone. They're both retired now, but they still live on the family farm. NeeNee moved in with them after my grandfather passed away."

"Hillstone is close to Edmonton, right?" Ivy said.

He nodded. "Edmonton is about two hours away. Have you been there?"

"A few elementary school trips to the West Ed Mall, and I did my animal health technology program at NAIT," Ivy said. "I haven't been back in years, though. So, um," her tone turned casual, "what about past relationships? Anything noteworthy?"

"Not really," he said. "I didn't date much in high school, too busy helping out with the farm. I dated a woman named Angela while I was in vet school – she was a fellow student – but it wasn't anything serious. She moved to Calgary after we finished school, and with me in Toronto, long-distance relationships are hard to maintain."

"Did you date anyone in Toronto?"

"A few different women over the years. Again, nothing serious. I've never brought a woman home to meet my parents before, which is why they're making such a big deal about meeting you."

"So," she poked at the chicken on her plate, "you know you'll have to tell them eventually that we're not getting married, right?"

"I know," he said. "I'll wait until after the holidays, maybe take some time off near the end of January to visit them and break the news."

"You're worried about how your NeeNee will take it, huh?"

He could hear the sympathy in her voice. God, he loved how sweet she was. "Yes, but that's my problem. I'm the grown-ass adult who decided that lying was the best option, and now I need to face the consequences."

"Do you want me to be awful when I'm there so that they'll hate me?" The look on her face was one of utter seriousness. "I could be rude and disrespectful, act like a total bitch to you, so they'll be happy we break up."

"I appreciate the thought, but I don't think you could be rude and disrespectful even if you tried," he said.

"I might," she said.

He laughed. "Doubtful. But thank you for the offer."

She took a sip of water and sat back in her chair. "Well, at the very least, tell them that I was the one who ended it. That way, I'm the jerk who broke your heart, and they hate me and feel bad for you."

"Hmm," he said teasingly, "I like that idea."

She laughed. "I'm full of good ideas on how to fake break up with your fake fiancée."

"What about your past relationships?" he asked.

"Dismal," she said. "I dated the quarterback in high school, that tragically ended when he was caught making out with the head cheerleader behind the bleachers."

"Wow, that is…"

"So cliché, right?" she said with a small laugh. "I managed not to be too traumatized by it, other than being self-conscious about the size of my boobs from that moment on."

It took an incredible amount of willpower not to drop his gaze to her chest. "What do you mean?"

"He told me he basically *had* to make out with Mandy because she was a D cup, and my boobs were too small to do it for him."

"Asshole," Elias said.

She shrugged. "He might have been the first boyfriend to complain about my small breasts, but he certainly hasn't been the last."

He couldn't help it. He glanced at her chest. In his mind, he could still see how beautiful they were with their soft, pale skin and pink nipples. Heat unfurling in his stomach, he said, "I think they're perfect."

She didn't reply, and he dragged his gaze to her face. Her cheeks were tinged pink, and she looked adorably flustered. "Um, sorry? What?"

He stared directly into her gorgeous green eyes. "I think they're perfect. From their perfect size to their perfect pink nipples, to the sweet little sounds you make when I suck on those perfect pink nipples."

She released her breath on a soft moan. It reminded him of the sounds she'd made last night, and his semi became a full-blown erection. "Ivy, maybe we should reconsider -"

"How's everything?" the server asked in a chirpy voice. "Need some water refills?"

He and Ivy sat back, identical guilty looks on their faces

as the server held up the water jug and stared expectantly at them.

"Um, yes, please," Ivy said. She dabbed at her mouth with her napkin and waited until the server left to meet his gaze. "Elias, I -"

"I'm sorry," he said. "Shit, that was, I mean... I shouldn't have... I apologize."

"Me too," she said.

"You have nothing to apologize for. I was being inappropriate."

"It's okay," she said hastily. "It was actually, um, a very lovely compliment, so, thank you."

His smile was strained. "You're welcome."

They sat in awkward silence for a few minutes before Ivy said. "Anyway, I did a bit of casual dating when I was doing my vet tech course, but nothing serious. And nothing really serious since either. With my job and the rescue, it doesn't leave a lot of time for dating."

"What about Ray Dorchester?" he asked, and immediately regretted it when a mask dropped over Ivy's face.

"What about him?" she said.

"I thought you two dated for a while. Am I wrong?"

He knew he wasn't. He'd spent the six months that Ivy dated Ray in a state of perpetual annoyance. The annoyance grew by leaps and bounds whenever he had the displeasure of seeing Ray pick Ivy up from work. He hated admitting how happy he was the day he overheard Ivy telling another of the vet techs that she and Ray had broken up.

But, yeah, you keep telling yourself it's just a crush on Ivy. Idiot.

"You're not wrong." Ivy tapped her fingers along the edge of the table and fidgeted in her chair. "We dated, but it wasn't serious."

"Didn't you date for, like, six months?" he asked.

"Yes. It was a mistake to date him, and I'd prefer not to talk about it." Her voice was now as flat and dull as the butter knife she was tapping against her plate.

"All right," he said.

More awkward silence, and then Ivy put her napkin over her half-eaten dinner. "It's getting late, and I still have to do laundry and pack for tomorrow. Do you mind if we call it a night?"

"Sure," he said. "Look, I'm sorry I -"

She shook her head. "It's all good. We can chat some more about personal stuff on the drive tomorrow, right?"

"Yes," he said.

"Great." Ivy fidgeted in her chair again, her gaze on her plate.

Shit. He'd fucked up again.

With an inward sigh, he flagged down the server.

Maybe if he reminded himself every damn hour, he'd remember that he wasn't actually dating Ivy and that everything happening between them was fake.

CHAPTER 8

"That's a lot of Christmas lights." Ivy unclicked her seatbelt, smiling a little when Bella leaned in from the back seat and licked across her cheek.

"Bella, no." Elias gave her a gentle push back. "My mom loves Christmas, so my dad always goes a little crazy with the decorations."

Ivy studied the house in front of her. It was a typical Alberta two-story farmhouse with white plank siding and a covered porch. Coloured lights were strung along the edge of the roof, around each of the windows, and along the edge of the porch roof. More lights wound around the pillar supports for the porch and the railing, a giant wreath adorned the wide front door, and lights twinkled in the two trees that flanked the house.

To the right of Elias's SUV, barely visible in the dark, loomed a building that Ivy assumed was the barn. "That's the barn, right?" she asked as Elias shut off the vehicle.

"Yes. I'll give you a tour tomorrow if you're interested."

"I am," she said. "Does your family still have cows?"

He nodded. "Not for work purposes, though. They're out

of the dairy business. Any of the cows Dad has now are his pets."

She laughed. "Really?"

"Yep. He loves cows. He's forever going to the auction and buying the ones that no one wants. He usually finds them good homes with neighbours, but he also keeps a fair share for himself. Mom says it drives her crazy, but secretly I'm pretty sure she loves how soft-hearted he is."

"That's adorable," she said.

He smiled at her, and she ignored the way it made her pulse kick up a notch. The entire drive here had been an exercise in willpower not to touch him. She stared at his ass when he climbed out of the SUV. Did he have to wear such tight jeans? And why did he have to smell so damn good?

"Are you coming?" Elias had turned around, and she quickly lifted her gaze from what was now his crotch.

"Yes, sorry."

"It'll be fine," he said. "I promise."

She climbed out of the SUV and, avoiding the deep snow, skirted around the vehicle to the back. Bella was already racing toward the front porch, barking with excitement, as Elias pulled both their suitcases out and closed the hatch.

"I'll carry it," he said when she reached for hers. "Be careful, it looks a bit slippery."

She followed him to the house, walking gingerly and staring at his perfect ass again. The front door opened, and Bella jumped up on the man standing in the doorway.

"Who's a good girl?" The man said as he rubbed Bella's head. "You're a good girl. Yes, you are. You're the best girl."

"Bella down. Hey, Dad," Elias climbed the steps of the porch. Holding onto the handrail and plastering a large smile on her face, Ivy followed.

"Elias. Welcome home, son." His father had silver-flecked

hair and a friendly smile, and he was as tall and muscular as Elias. He wrapped Elias in his embrace and pounded him on the back. "How was the drive?"

"Good. Roads were a bit slippery, but not terrible. Dad, this is my fiancée, Ivy. Ivy, this is my dad, Doug."

Ivy held out her hand. "It's nice to meet you, Mr. Hart."

Doug grinned at her before shaking her hand enthusiastically. "It's so great to meet you, Ivy. Please, call me Doug." His face lit up. "Or Dad! You could call me Dad. You're part of the family now, after all."

"Dad," Elias said. "Remember what we talked about."

Doug turned to Ivy. "He made me promise to rein in my enthusiasm over meeting you, and not be… weird. I said I would. Am I being weird?"

"You are *now*," Elias said.

Ivy laughed. "You're not being weird."

"See, Elias. I'm not being weird." Doug ushered Ivy inside, and Elias followed with the suitcases.

Doug took the suitcases from him. "Your mother and grandmother are in the kitchen. Introduce them to Ivy while I take these upstairs."

"Thanks, Dad," Elias said.

Doug walked down the narrow hallway to the stairs at the end. As he climbed the stairs, Bella at his heels, Ivy and Elias took off their boots and hung their jackets on the hooks on the wall behind the door.

"It smells delicious in here," Ivy said.

Elias nodded. "Smells like Mom made stew for dinner."

Ivy's stomach growled in response, and Elias smiled down at her. "C'mon, let's get you some of my mom's world-famous stew."

"Right," she said. Nerves were suddenly replacing the hunger pangs.

As if he sensed it, Elias took her hand and squeezed it. "You okay?"

"Just nervous."

"You've got this," he said.

She lowered her voice to just above a whisper. "I'm nervous about messing this up or accidentally blurting out the truth. Remember, I can't lie worth shit."

"You'll be good," he said with a confidence she envied. "Instead of thinking about how we're supposed to be in love, just think about how attracted we are to each other. That's not a lie, right?"

"Right," she said.

He started toward the kitchen and, knowing she shouldn't, but dammit, she really wanted to, she said, "A kiss would help."

"What?"

"A kiss would help me, uh, get into character."

A slow smile crossed his face. "Is that right?"

"Yes." She stared at his mouth. "I mean, it's what people who are engaged do, right? They kiss."

"They do," he said.

She shivered when he backed her up against the wall, his hand dropping to her hip, the other resting on the wall next to her head. He studied her mouth, and when he bent his head and pressed his lips against hers, she parted her lips immediately.

He skimmed his tongue along her bottom lip before angling his mouth over hers and taking the kiss deeper. She clutched at his waist, her body arching toward his as they kissed.

God, her boss really was the best kisser.

She forgot about her nervousness as Elias's tongue dipped between her lips. He stroked her tongue with his, his hand tightening on her hip when she moaned into his mouth.

"Elias?"

He pulled away from her, clearing his throat and turning to smile at the blonde woman standing in a doorway a few feet away. "Hey, Mom."

"Hi, honey."

Mortified, Ivy pushed away from Elias and tried to smile at the woman as she walked toward her. She held out her hand. "Hi there. I'm Ivy. I'm, uh, Elias's, um…"

"Fiancée," the woman said. "It's nice to meet you. I'm Barbara."

Ivy shook her hand, wishing that her cheeks weren't quite the fiery red she knew they were. "It's really lovely to meet you. Elias has told me so much about you and the rest of his family."

"Has he?" Barbara said. "That's nice. He hasn't really told us very much about you at all."

Her nerves stringing tighter, Ivy said, "Well, I hope we can remedy that over the next few days, Mrs. Hart."

Elias's mother studied her for a moment before nodding. "I'd like that. Call me Barb. Are you hungry?"

"We are," Elias said. "We had to work late at the clinic and didn't have time to eat before we drove here."

"We ate earlier, but I've set aside some stew for you and Ivy. Come into the kitchen and meet NeeNee, while I heat it up," Barb said.

Ivy stepped into the warm kitchen. It was twice the size of her kitchen at home, featuring an old but solid-looking oak table tucked up against a big bay window, and a butcher block-topped island with three stools in front of the bank of white cabinets. Stainless steel appliances gleamed, and the entire kitchen was decorated in a rooster and blue and white checkered theme. It was the quintessential farmhouse kitchen, Ivy decided.

Elias had already walked over to the older woman sitting at the table. He leaned down, embracing her with a kiss on the cheek and a warm smile. "Hi, NeeNee."

"Hi, honey." The woman beamed at him. She looked like the storybook version of a grandmother, from the carefully curled fine white hair and kind blue eyes down to the cane she held and the orthopedic shoes she wore on her feet.

Taking a deep breath, Ivy joined them. Elias took her hand, and she was grateful for his silent support as she smiled at his grandmother. "Hello, I'm Ivy."

"Ivy." Elias's grandmother looked her up and down, her soft smile growing larger. "It's so nice to meet you. You're as pretty as Elias said you were."

"And you're as beautiful as he told me you were," Ivy said.

His grandmother laughed. "He's always been a charmer, this one. Is that how he won your hand in marriage?"

Ivy nodded. "Definitely."

NeeNee's gaze drifted down to her left hand. "Did he give you the ring?"

Ivy held her hand out, warmth settling in her chest when NeeNee stared at the ring on her hand and immediately teared up.

"Don't cry, NeeNee. Let me get you a tissue." Elias walked away as NeeNee took Ivy's hand.

Ivy crouched in front of her, and NeeNee patted her cheek. "You are a sweet girl to wear this ring."

"I love it," Ivy said. She wasn't lying. She'd only been wearing it since they started the drive, but she loved the simplicity of the ring, and it already felt… right to wear it.

NeeNee patted her cheek again. "The diamond is non-existent, and it's probably not as pretty as the ones they have now, but it meant so much to me and to my husband. To know that the woman our Elias loves is wearing it..."

The tears slipped down her cheeks, following the grooves and lines that time had worn into her face. "It's just very special to see you wearing it."

Guilt was starting to wind its way through Ivy's belly. She pushed it down as Elias returned and handed a tissue to his grandmother. "Here, NeeNee."

"Thank you, sweetheart." NeeNee dabbed at her face before squeezing Ivy's hand. "Ivy, you must sit beside me and tell me all about the night that Elias proposed. I bet it was so romantic."

Panic replaced the guilt. They hadn't come up with a cover story for the proposal. Shit! Why hadn't they come up with a cover story for the proposal?

"NeeNee, Ivy's tired and hungry," Elias said as his mother placed bowls of steaming hot stew and a plate of fresh biscuits on the table.

He helped Ivy stand and pulled the chair out next to NeeNee. Ivy sat down and spooned some stew into her mouth. It was piping hot, and the bites of potato, carrot, and beef swimming in rich gravy tasted a little bit like heaven to her. "This is incredible, Barb."

"Thank you. Have some biscuits as well. I made them fresh tonight," Barb said. "NeeNee, did you hear that the McKellens' girl had another baby?"

"Okay, suitcases are upstairs." Doug joined them in the kitchen and sat down next to Barb.

Bella, her bum wiggling, was already leaning against NeeNee, staring adoringly at her. NeeNee petted her lightly, her fingers weaving through the hair on Bella's back.

Ivy and Elias ate silently as Barb, Doug, and NeeNee talked about various families in the town. Elias slipped his hand under the table and rested it on her thigh. She found his touch reassuring, and when he squeezed her leg and smiled encouragingly at her, she returned his smile.

"This stew is amazing," she said in a low voice.

He leaned in close. "Right? I told you my mom was an awesome cook."

"You were not wrong," she said with a small grin before scraping her bowl clean.

"Did you want more, Ivy?" Barb asked.

"Thank you, but I'm full," Ivy said. "It was delicious."

"Maybe you could tell us how our boy proposed now?" NeeNee said eagerly.

Elias's hand tightened on her thigh. "Tomorrow, NeeNee. Ivy is still tired and -"

"Nonsense," Barb said. "It'll only take a few minutes. Go on, Ivy, I'd love to hear the story too."

"Oh, um, well…" Ivy couldn't look up from her empty bowl. If she did, his mother would see the panic in her eyes. "It wasn't actually, I mean, that is…"

Why the heck wasn't Elias jumping in to save her? When the quiet turned awkward, Ivy blurted, "It was at the clinic. After work. A feral cat had just peed on me, and I turned around, and Elias was on his knee with the ring in his hand."

The silence was deafening. "Um, I still found it really romantic though."

"I meant to propose before she got peed on," Elias said.

Another moment of pure silence before Elias's dad started to giggle. Nerves and the hilarious high-pitched sound coming out of such a big man gave Ivy her own immediate fit of giggles. Doug laughed harder at the sound of Ivy's giggles, and neither NeeNee nor Barb could keep a straight face.

"Meant to propose before she got peed on," Doug gasped out. "Oh my God, son."

"What?" Elias grinned at him. "You think I meant to propose while my girlfriend smelled like cat pee?"

"Oh, honey," Barb wiped away the tears of laughter. "You really need to work on your romantic side. Poor Ivy."

She stood, and when she reached for Ivy's bowl, Ivy stood as well. Still giggling, she said, "I can clean up."

"No, no," Barb said. "It's late, and I'm sure you're both tired from the trip. Go on upstairs, and we'll see you in the morning. Elias, honey, I put fresh sheets on your bed, and there are towels in the bathroom. You remember how chilly it can get upstairs, so if you need extra blankets, grab them from the linen closet."

Ivy's giggles dried up instantly. She and Elias would be sharing a bed.

Uh, duh. Did you think you wouldn't be?

She hadn't thought of it, to be honest. She'd been too wrapped up in worrying that she would blow their story to think about details like where they'd be sleeping and if she'd be lying next to Elias's warm, hard body all night.

Her core tingled pleasantly at the thought, and she glared at her crotch. *Stop it right now, you hussy!*

Elias's hand was suddenly in hers, and he tugged her toward the doorway of the kitchen. "Good night, everyone. Bella, come."

The dog remained seated at Doug's feet, and Elias rolled his eyes. "Seriously? Already?"

He turned to Ivy. "She loves my dad more than she loves me."

Doug laughed and petted Bella's head. "She can sleep in our room tonight. Good night, you guys."

They escaped into the hallway and, still holding her hand,

Elias led her up the stairs. Her nerve ends buzzing and her knees rattling, Ivy followed him into the bedroom. The room was tastefully decorated in blues and grays with white shiplap walls.

She swallowed hard. The bed was a queen-size with a wrought-iron headboard and footboard. It would be fine. Elias was on the large side, but she wasn't. There would be plenty of room in the bed. They wouldn't have to touch at all.

That thought sent a weird tingle of dismay down her spine.

"Um, this is nice," she said.

"It was my room growing up," Elias said. "Mom redid it into more of a guest room, though. So, no more Led Zeppelin and Pink Floyd posters."

She smiled up at him. "Big classic rock fan, huh?"

"Yeah, my dad loves it, and he got me into it at an early age." He glanced at their clasped hands and abruptly dropped her hand. "So, uh, I'll sleep on the floor."

"What?" Ivy said.

"You can have the bed," he said.

"You're going to sleep on the floor?" Ivy stared at the hardwood floor beneath their feet. "But it's hardwood."

"It's fine. I'm not expecting you to share a bed with me." He pointed to the door to their right. "That's the attached bathroom. Are you good if I use it first?"

She nodded, and he grabbed his toiletry bag from his suitcase and headed to the bathroom. She unzipped her suitcase and unpacked her pajamas and her toiletry bag. During packing the night before, Bryce had forbidden her to pack her robe, but Ivy put the kybosh on the sexy little chemise Bryce tried to convince her to pack. Instead, she'd packed her not-at-all-sexy but very practical cotton shorts and t-shirt pajamas.

She heard the bathroom door open. "You don't have to sleep on the floor, Elias."

Elias paused by his open suitcase. "It's all good, Ivy. I'm not expecting you to share a bed with me."

"You already said that." She could hear the irritation creeping into her voice. "It's no big deal. It's a big bed and we're both adults. You stay on your side and I'll stay on my side. I think we can manage to share the same bed without..."

"Without what?" he said.

Without me jumping you like a horny teenage girl.

"Without it being a big deal," she said.

"Are you sure?" He glanced at the bed and then back at her.

"Positive. As long as you're all right with sleeping on the left side because I'm claiming the right."

An easy grin crossed his face. "I can live with that."

"Good." Holding her toiletry bag and pajamas, she marched past him to the bathroom.

She washed her face, brushed and flossed her teeth, and then changed into her pajamas. She hesitated about removing her bra before rolling her eyes at her reflection in the mirror. Elias had already seen her boobs. It was no big deal to go braless.

He's seen one boob. One boob, Ivy. Maybe you should show him the other one while you're in bed with him, just to be fair.

She ignored her inner voice. She wasn't showing Elias *anything* in the bed. She opened the bathroom door and walked back into the bedroom. She was crawling into bed to get some sleep, and absolutely, positively, nothing else was going to hap...

"Holy mother of God," she breathed quietly.

Elias had turned off the overhead light, and she stared hungrily at his naked back in the dim light of the bedside lamp as he zipped up his suitcase. He was wearing a pair of pajama bottoms that sat low on his hips, and she studied his delectable ass.

He turned around, and she soaked in the beautiful sight of a half-naked Elias. He looked just as good as she remembered. Hell, even better, now that the scratches on his chest and back were mostly healed.

"Ivy?"

She dragged her gaze away from his six-pack. "Yeah?"

"You sure about the bed thing?"

"I am." Her voice sounded weird, even to herself. "No big deal, right?"

He didn't reply, and she dropped her clothes on top of her suitcase, then hurried to the bed and climbed in. She yanked the quilt and the sheet up to her chin and turned on her side away from Elias. The bed dipped as he got in. The room and the bed were cold, and she stared at the shadows on the wall, resisting the urge to scoot over and leech some of his body heat from him.

"Sorry about the proposal story," she said. "I panicked."

He laughed. "It's all good."

"I told you I couldn't lie."

"You did fine for being put on the spot like that. It's my fault for not preparing you. I should have known NeeNee would ask about the proposal."

She wanted to roll over and face him, but didn't dare. If she saw him lying there half-naked, she might be tempted to do *things* to him. Instead, she clutched the sheets even tighter around her, trying not to shiver.

"Sorry, it's a bit chilly," he said. "It's an old house and not well-insulated."

"It's fine." She buried her cold nose under the quilt. "Good night, Elias."

He shut off the light. "Good night, Ivy."

CHAPTER 9

Waking up with Ivy's soft body plastered against his back and her arm and leg draped over him was not the worst way to wake up. In fact, if his dick was to be believed, it was the *best* way to wake up.

Elias glanced at the alarm clock. It was well after nine, and the bedroom was soaked in cold sunlight. He stared at Ivy's hand resting against his chest. The tiny diamond on her engagement ring sparkled in the light.

Not her engagement ring.

It was hard to remember that his relationship with Ivy was fake when Ivy's soft warmth was tucked up against him, and his morning wood was screaming for relief. He'd been worried that he wouldn't stay on his side of the bed during the night, but apparently it was Ivy who liked to snuggle.

She's just cold. It doesn't mean anything.

No, probably not. Which is why he needed to get out of bed before he did something stupid like kiss her awake.

He tried to ease out of the bed, muttering a curse under his breath when Ivy's grip immediately tightened around him. Christ, for how little she was, she was stronger than she looked.

He tried again, and Ivy wiggled even closer. She kissed his back and mumbled, "No, honey. Stay in bed."

He froze when her hand slipped down his chest and rested against his aching dick. She sighed happily behind him, her warm breath making goosebumps pop up along his spine, before rubbing him lightly through his pajamas.

"Ivy, wake up," he said.

She mumbled something he didn't understand and rubbed harder.

"Ivy, you need to wake up now."

He gave up trying to escape her and rolled to face her instead. She smiled sleepily at him and snuggled in close, tucking her head up into his chest and pressing her hand against his dick again.

"Let's have a quickie," she muttered.

Oh hell, yes.

"Ivy, open your eyes," he croaked out. It was growing increasingly difficult to keep his hands to himself.

She leaned back, squinting up at him. "What's wrong?"

"Um…" he looked down at his crotch, at the way her hand cupped him, and she followed his gaze.

"Oh my God." She snatched her hand back, her eyes wide and horrified, as she stared up at him. "I'm so sorry."

He should have told her it was no big deal and gotten the hell out of the bed. Instead, he rasped, "I'm not."

Her cheeks were flushed, and she studied his mouth before abruptly pressing her lips against his. He groaned and immediately rolled her to her back, pushing his thigh between hers and covering her body with his, pressing her deep into the mattress as he took control of the kiss.

She gasped when he nipped at her throat and slipped his

hand under her shirt to cup one perfect breast. Her nipple was hard against his palm, and he rubbed his thumb across it, smiling when she made a low cry of need.

"Elias, please," she moaned.

He reached for the hem of her shirt, and she helped him pull it over her head. She arched her back when he skimmed his hand along her ribs and kissed between her breasts. Her hands gripped his hair, and she guided his mouth to her nipple. He gave her what she wanted, sucking and licking at both her nipples until they were swollen, and their pink colour had deepened to a dark rose.

She rocked her pelvis against his hardness, her slender thighs wrapped around his as her fingertips traced light circles around the healing scratches on his back.

"I want you, Ivy," he said in a low voice.

"I want you too," she gasped. Her hands dipped to his ass and squeezed. He pressed his dick against her hip and traced the waistband of her shorts.

"You sure?" He tasted the hollow of her throat.

"Yes," she squeezed his ass again, "touch me before I go insane."

He grinned against her throat, his hand slipping under the waistband of her shorts. He cupped her warmth, fresh desire flooding his body. "You're so wet, Ivy."

"Please," she moaned.

He kissed her again, swallowing her loud cry of pleasure when he rubbed her swollen clit with the pad of his thumb.

He couldn't get enough of her reaction, of her kisses, of her warm touch. He could spend the rest of his life in bed with Ivy, and it still wouldn't be long enough.

He pressed a kiss against the fluttering pulse in her throat and circled his fingers harder and faster. He would make Ivy come, and then he'd bury himself in her tight warmth and find the release he'd been craving since the moment he met her. She would finally be his, and he would be hers and –

The knock at his bedroom door made them both jerk in surprise. He pulled his hand from beneath her shorts, and Ivy tugged the quilt up to her neck. They gave each other identical looks of guilt as his father said through the door, "Elias, you awake?"

"Yeah." Elias cleared his throat. "We, uh, we just woke up."

"Good. Come downstairs then. Your mother made French toast for breakfast, and it's just about ready."

"We'll be right there," Elias said. Ivy yanked her shirt over her head and scooted to her side of the bed as his father's footsteps faded down the hall.

"I'm sorry," Elias said.

She huffed out a humourless laugh as she slid out of bed. "I'm the one who needs to apologize. It was my fault. I started it."

He didn't reply as she pulled a sweatshirt out of her suitcase and grabbed her toiletry bag. "Do you, um, mind if I use the bathroom first?"

He shook his head, collapsing onto the mattress and staring up at the ceiling as Ivy hurried into the bathroom and shut the door.

"You didn't have to wait to decorate the tree," Elias said.

"Of course, we did." Barb handed him a box of ornaments before smiling at Ivy. "It's tradition. We always decorate the tree together."

"That's a lovely tradition." Ivy held the ornament NeeNee had given her and watched as Doug helped his mother place an ornament on the tree before she shuffled to a chair by the fire. It was a wood fireplace, and Ivy loved the sound of the wood crackling and popping.

"What are your family Christmas traditions?" Barb asked. Her gaze switched between Ivy and Elias, and the thoughtful look on her face made Ivy nervous.

His mother knew something was wrong. Knew it the very second she and Elias had joined them in the kitchen. With the awkwardness that was radiating between her and Elias in thick, heavy waves, Ivy supposed she should be grateful that neither Doug nor NeeNee had sensed it.

Or maybe they had, and the entire family knew this was a complete sham. Any minute now, they were going to demand to know the truth, and she would crack under the pressure, and Elias would never forgive her and probably fire her, or worse, never speak to her again.

Pull it together, Ivy!

Yes, she needed to do exactly that. She'd been avoiding touching Elias all morning, hell, she could barely look him in the eye, and sooner or later, more than his mother would notice.

So, she had accidentally groped her boss, no biggie, right? Probably everyone had accidentally groped their boss at some point in their life. He'd been into it, just as much as she was, and sometimes when two adults shared a bed... stuff happened.

Stuff happened all right. Good job on showing him both your boobs this time.

Her inner voice was practically crowing with delight.

She took a deep breath. She could do this. She could play the part of the perfect fiancée. Elias had already written off the debt to the rescue and bought the new microwave for the break room. She would hold up her end of the deal. She would act like she was madly in love with him, and she would be affectionate and touchy-feely with him in front of his parents, like a fiancée would do.

Even if it left her so horny she could barely see straight.

"Ivy?" Barb prompted. "Are you all right?"

"Yes, sorry." Ivy hung the ornament on the tree and reached for another. "In our house, we open a present on Christmas Eve, and we watch *Die Hard*."

"That's Elias's favourite movie," Doug said.

"I know," Ivy said even though she didn't. She walked over to Elias and put her arms around his waist before standing on her tiptoes and pressing a light kiss against his mouth. "Our mutual love for *Die Hard* was one of the reasons we started dating. Isn't that right, honey?"

"Yes," Elias agreed.

Ivy kept her arm around his waist and leaned against his side, hoping it looked like this was a natural, everyday occurrence. It helped when Elias put his arm around her and leaned down to give her another kiss.

"Oh, you two are just so sweet," NeeNee said from her spot by the fire. "It warms my heart to see you so happy. Thank you for joining us, Ivy. I'm sure it wasn't easy leaving your family at Christmas."

Ivy smiled at her. "I really wanted to meet all of you, and luckily, my Nana has a friend who she's spending Christmas with."

"Your parents are in Victoria, is that right?" Barb asked.

"They are. They're coming for a visit in February," Ivy said.

"Maybe we'll drive down to meet them," Barb said.

"Mom," Elias said.

"What? We'd love to meet Ivy's parents. They're going to be our family after all," Barb said.

"I know, but they'll probably be busy doing…stuff," he said.

Good gravy, Elias was a worse liar than she was.

She squeezed his waist and said, "That sounds great. I know my folks will love meeting you, too."

"Good," Barb said. "Now, let's hurry and finish up decorating the tree. We need to leave soon."

"Leave for where?" Elias asked.

"Didn't your father tell you?" Barb glanced at Doug, who shrugged sheepishly. "The town brought back the annual Christmas Eve potluck and sleigh ride this year."

"What?" Elias glanced at Ivy. "Are you serious?"

Barb nodded. "I am. The potluck starts at two, and the sleigh rides start at four. We have tickets for the 5:00 and 5:30 slots. It'll be the perfect opportunity to introduce Ivy to everyone."

Elias was looking decidedly panicked. When his mother walked away to hang up another ornament, he said in a loud voice, "Oh, you're thirsty, Ivy? Come into the kitchen, I'll make you a coffee."

He hurried her out of the living room, and once they were in the kitchen, Ivy said in a low voice, "What's wrong?"

"Half the damn town shows up for this thing," he said. "They'll all be asking us questions!"

She decided a panicking Elias was an adorable Elias.

"Don't stress about it," she said. "As long as we stick together so we can keep our answers straight on whatever questions they ask, we'll be fine."

He stared down at her. "What happened to the 'I can't lie worth crap and I'm going to blow the whole thing,' Ivy, that I know and love?"

Love?

Don't read into it, she told herself. *It's just an expression.*

"I don't know, to be honest. I mean, I'm still a little worried that I'll blurt out the truth, but I also promised to help you, and I intend to keep that promise. So, we put on our best 'we're in love' faces and keep our answers short and simple. Right?" she said.

"Right," he said.

He took her hand when she tried to leave, tugging her to a stop. "Ivy, about this morning..."

She sighed. "Now it's my turn to apologize for the inappropriateness. I'm sorry, Elias."

"I don't want you to be sorry," he said. He pulled her even closer and studied her mouth.

She was suddenly very aware of how good he smelled, of how deliciously warm his body was. She could smell the mint on his breath from the peppermint tea he'd been drinking as he bent his head.

"What do you want?" she whispered.

"I want you to admit that you want me as much as I want you. I want you to admit that if we hadn't been interrupted this morning, we wouldn't have stopped."

She swallowed heavily, studying the curve of his very suckable bottom lip. Her voice was a barely discernible whisper. "We wouldn't have stopped."

His nostrils flared, and when he kissed her, she returned his kiss eagerly. He leaned against the counter, spreading his legs and pulling her in between them. He cupped her ass, kissing her with a slow type of determination that set her skin on fire with need.

He broke the kiss to allow her to gasp in a breath of air before he kissed her again. His tongue teased hers, and she crowded up against him as he squeezed and kneaded her ass.

His dad stuck his head into the kitchen. "Hey, buddy, can you get some tea for Nee... oops. Sorry."

Elias let go of her ass, but when she tried to move away, he put his arm around her waist, keeping her pinned against him.

His father grinned at them. "So, should I get the tea or…"

Her cheeks red, Ivy studied Elias's broad chest as he said, "Tea for NeeNee. Got it."

"Thanks, buddy."

His dad left, and Ivy groaned out a curse. "Your dad has the worst timing."

"Tell me about it." Elias let her go. "Sorry I didn't let you go, but I wasn't keen on my father seeing the damn semi I'm sporting."

He pulled at the crotch of his jeans, and Ivy was weirdly pleased by the noticeable bulge.

"We should get the tea and get back to decorating the tree before my mother and my grandmother come in here as well," Elias said.

What Ivy really wanted was to coax him upstairs and strip him naked so she could do all the delicious things to him she'd been dreaming about for months. Instead, she manufactured a smile and nodded. "Sounds like a plan."

CHAPTER 10

Ivy tugged on his hand, and when he bent his head, she whispered, "It's going well."

"It is. I think we might be in the clear." Elias pulled her a little closer, partly to keep her warm and partly because he loved touching her. They were waiting in the cold air for their turn on the sleigh, and he pasted a smile on his face when Loralee Walters puffed her way up to them.

"There you are!" She eyed the way his arm was wrapped around Ivy's shoulders. "Why, if I didn't know better, Elias Hart, I'd say you've been avoiding me all afternoon."

He had, as a matter of fact, been avoiding her. It wasn't that he didn't like Loralee, but she was the nosiest person in town, and she wouldn't be content with the short and straightforward answers that he and Ivy had been giving to everyone else.

No, she would want every single detail of how they'd met, and while her body might be getting up there in age, her mind was not. She'd point out holes in their story faster than Bella snatched a piece of bacon out of the air.

"You're a tiny little thing, aren't you?" Loralee said to Ivy. "You work with Elias, do you?"

"That's right," Ivy said. She held out one mitten-covered hand. "I'm Ivy West. It's nice to meet you."

"Loralee, nice to meetcha' as well. You've been dating Elias how long now?" Loralee asked.

"A while now," Ivy said. "How do you know Elias?"

"I volunteer with his mama in the church nursery," Loralee said. "When are you getting married?"

"We haven't set a date yet," Ivy said. "I love your hat and scarf combo. They look homemade."

Loralee puffed with pride. "Knitted them myself."

"Beautiful craftsmanship," Ivy said. "Have you been knitting long?"

As Ivy steered Loralee into a conversation about knitting, Elias's admiration for her deepened. It'd been like this from the moment they showed up. He dutifully introduced Ivy to everyone who approached them, they would ask a few questions, and Ivy would find a way to steer the conversation to being about them. It was a brilliant plan, and he couldn't wait to get Ivy alone and tell her how much he appreciated her outside of the box thinking.

Maybe you could show her how much you appreciate it.

Warmth infused his belly. Showing Ivy exactly how much he appreciated everything she was doing to help him was an idea he couldn't seem to let go of. Especially since that moment in bed this morning.

They'd be alone in the bed again tonight. An image of Ivy, naked with her legs spread wide and her soft voice begging him to take her, lodged itself permanently in his brain. He closed his eyes and counted to ten. He was *not* getting a stiffy at a damn town social function.

Tell that to your dick.

He could hear the jingling of the bells on the sleigh, and Ivy's hand tightened in his. "You okay?"

"Fine." He opened his eyes, pulling Ivy back a little as the horses, their breath steaming out in the cold air, trotted by them. The sleigh, one of two that his dad had helped build back in the nineties, stopped in front of them. The sleigh riders climbed out, their cheeks red and their voices excited as they headed to the community center behind them for hot chocolate.

"When are you planning on having kids?" Loralee asked.

"Sorry, Loralee, we have tickets for the five-thirty ride," Elias said as he pulled Ivy toward the sleigh. "Good to see you again."

Elias handed their tickets to the volunteer, and he and Ivy approached the sleigh. It was painted red and gold, featuring four bench seats and a designated spot at the front for the driver. Elias boosted Ivy into the last bench of the sleigh, his hands lingering around her waist. Not that he could feel anything through the thick winter jacket she was wearing, but he liked how her cheeks flushed and her eyes turned bright whenever he touched her.

He climbed in after her, and they slid to the end. He nodded to the couple who climbed in after them. Miracles of miracles, he had no idea who they were, and he was thankful he wouldn't have to make small talk. He wanted to concentrate on Ivy.

The sleigh filled up quickly, and as the driver called to the horses and the sleigh slid smoothly through the snow, Elias put his arm around Ivy.

She smiled up at him. "This is fun."

"I'm glad you like it. Are you warm enough?"

She nodded, patting her thick jacket and readjusting her scarf and hat. "Yep. I made sure to layer."

His gaze dropped to her mouth. "Are you sure? Your lips look a little blue."

They weren't. They were their normal soft pink colour, but he was dying to kiss her.

She cocked her head at him, a hint of laughter on her face. "Is that right?"

"Maybe I should warm them up."

"Maybe you should."

He pressed his mouth against hers, loving the way her mitten-clad hands curled into his jacket and pulled him even closer. He was tempted to take the kiss deeper, but pulled back instead. Shoving his tongue down Ivy's throat on the sleigh ride would definitely be inappropriate.

She smiled up at him before leaning against him and watching the trees as the sleigh carried them on a loop through the woods. Some volunteers had decorated the path with lights, and Ivy sighed contentedly. "It's so pretty."

"You're pretty," he said, then groaned at how cheesy he sounded.

Her smile widened, and he was very glad he'd blurted out the cheesy line. "Thank you."

She studied him for a few moments. "I really like your family. They're lovely, and I can see why you did what you did when it came to your NeeNee. She's special."

"She is," he said. "Thank you again for everything."

"You're welcome."

Unable to resist her sweetness, he pressed another kiss against her mouth before settling back in the sleigh. Being with Ivy, touching her, and pretending to be engaged was way easier than it should have been.

He studied the lights glimmering on the trees. Just the thought of returning to a normal relationship with her filled him with anxiety and unease. Maybe once they returned home, he could ask her about dating.

Really? She's your employee. What if something goes wrong, you break up, and she quits? She's the most competent tech you have. Don't start thinking this is real. It isn't, and as soon as you're back home, this whole charade ends. You'll never touch or kiss Ivy again.

"Elias? You okay?" Ivy asked.

He nodded and pulled her a little closer. "I'm fine."

"Ivy, can you come into the living room for a minute?" Barb called.

"Be right there." She put her glass in the dishwasher and petted Bella's head when she leaned against her. "You're a good girl."

She headed toward the living room, Bella trailing behind her. Elias had been quiet and withdrawn since the sleigh ride, and she was worried about him. She'd racked her brain trying to think if she'd said or done anything to upset him, but kept coming up empty.

She would talk to him once they went to bed, she decided. Something was bothering him, and she was determined to find out what it was. Even if she had to –

She stopped in her tracks, staring at the television and the paused face of Bruce Willis in *Die Hard*. "What's this?"

Doug grinned at her from his easy chair by the fire. "Mom's gone to bed, but Barb and Elias and I wanted to honour one of your family traditions."

She could feel tears threatening, and she blinked rapidly as Elias took her hand and led her to the couch. She curled up next to him as Barb sat next to Doug in her matching easy chair.

"This is so nice of you," Ivy said. A tear slipped down her cheek, and Elias rubbed it away with his thumb.

"You're a part of our family now," Barb said. "Your traditions are our traditions."

"Thank you so much," Ivy said. "You've made me feel so welcome, and I'll never forget how kind you are."

"You're welcome, honey," Barb said. She patted Doug's hand. "Start the movie, sweetheart."

Elias put his arm around her, and she leaned into him, resting her hand on his thigh and rubbing lightly. He kissed the top of her head, and as they settled in to watch *Die Hard*, she tamped down both the guilt and the depression that were trying to creep past the happiness.

She had grown used to touching Elias, to kissing him whenever she wanted, and in two days it would end, and they'd be back to a working relationship only. Nausea swirled in her belly at the thought. Maybe it didn't have to end. Maybe they could try a relationship. There was an attraction between them, and she'd always found him smart and funny and kind. Why shouldn't they date for real?

Uh, maybe because if it goes bad, the rescue is screwed. I know you don't want to think that Elias would fire you or stop helping the rescue, but you didn't think Ray would convince his dad to stop donating either, did you?

Shit, she hated when inner Ivy was right.

"You okay?" Elias asked.

"Yeah. You?"

"Fine."

He didn't look fine, but now was not the time to push him about it. With a soft sigh, she concentrated on the movie.

———

IVY STARED UP AT THE CEILING. THE LIGHTS WERE OFF IN THE bedroom, but Doug had forgotten to shut off the outside Christmas lights, and they cast a soft glow in the bedroom. Enough that she could clearly see Elias's profile as he lay on his back beside her.

His breathing was slow and rhythmic, but she knew he wasn't sleeping. No, he was wide awake and staring at the ceiling, trying to ignore the sexual tension between them just like she was. She would never fall asleep.

Was it possible for someone to die because they were too horny?

Lying in the dark next to a half-naked Elias and not being allowed to touch him made her sure it was possible.

She needed to think of the bright side - dropping dead because she couldn't get laid would make for a hell of an obituary.

It's Christmas. Why shouldn't you give yourself a present? It doesn't have to mean anything. You could have sex tonight. In fact, it's probably a good idea to do it. The tension between you is notice-able, and sooner or later, his family will start asking questions.

Her inner voice made an excellent point. She could at least broach the subject with Elias. If they were both clear that it went no further than tonight and that it was simply a break the tension kind of deal, it would be fine. People had casual sex all the time. Why couldn't she and Elias do the same?

Sure, he was her boss, but she bet plenty of people had

seen their bosses naked. It was no big deal. They were adults and could keep it professional afterward. Right?

When sensible Ivy didn't weigh in with all the reasons her thinking was insane, Ivy cleared her throat and said, "Elias?"

"Yeah?"

"I was thinking maybe we should have sex."

Elias propped himself up on his elbows, the shock on his face easy to see. "What?"

Her face burning, she sat up and hugged her knees to her chest. "I think it would help to sell the relationship with your family."

He raised an eyebrow at her. "Just how loud are you during sex?"

Nervous giggles exploded from her mouth. "Not because they'll hear us, you dork. I just meant there's obvious tension between us, and your family is starting to notice. If we had sex, the tension would disappear, right?"

"Yes," he said. "But you're my employee and -"

"It's just casual sex," she said quickly. "We have sex tonight and ease the weird tension, and then we're good to go. I can keep it professional at work after this is done, I promise."

He stayed silent, and, her heart sinking, she said, "I'm sorry. I thought you would want this too. Forget I said anything."

He sat up next to her, shaking his head. "I do want this. I just want to make sure that you're okay with the casual sex concept."

"Why wouldn't I be? Because I'm a woman?" She rolled her eyes. "That's a sexist idea, Elias."

"You're right, it is. I apologize," he said. "But we did make an agreement that you helping me with my lie didn't require any type of sexual relationship, and I want to be positive that you know that hasn't changed. I can do a better job tomorrow of convincing my family that we're madly in love."

"Or we could have sex and the tension will disappear and neither of us has to work twice as hard to convince your family of anything," she said. "Let's take a vote on it – option A, we do a more convincing job of ignoring how badly we want to bang each other's brains out and convince your family we're the perfect couple, or option B, we bang each other's brains out."

A slow smile was crossing his face as she said, "All those in favour of option A, raise your hand."

He kept his hands in his lap, that smile becoming sinfully sexy as she said, "All those in favour of option B, raise your hand."

They stared at each other's hands raised in the air before Ivy said, "Two to zero. We basically have no choice now but to have sex."

"That sounds fair," he said.

She laughed and scooted a little closer. "You sure this is what you want?"

He studied her face in the dim light. "More than sure. I want you, Ivy. Very much."

"I want you too," she said.

He reached for her and paused when she said, "Hold that thought."

She hopped out of bed, goosebumps covering her skin almost immediately, and hurried over to her suitcase. She rummaged in the inside pocket before turning and showing him the handful of condoms.

He smiled at her. "Why, Ms. West, were you planning on seducing me all along?"

She blushed and climbed back into bed, placing the

condoms on the bedside table. "Bryce put them in the suit-case when I was packing as a 'just in case' scenario."

"God bless Bryce," he said so solemnly that she giggled again.

He cupped her face and leaned in, pressing a kiss against her mouth. "Nothing will change between us because of this, Ivy. I promise."

Everything will change.

"I know," she said.

He kissed her again, his touch slow and gentle as he traced the inner skin of her forearm with the tips of his fingers. She rested her hand on his chest, the rough feel of his chest hair and the warmth of his skin sending tingles of awareness up and down her spine.

He was still kissing her in that slow and thoughtful way that drove her mad with need. With a low groan of frustration, she pulled back and quickly yanked her pajama top over her head. His gaze immediately arrowed in on her chest, and she smiled inwardly when he cupped her breast and stroked her nipple into a hard point with his thumb.

She sank onto her back on the soft mattress, pulling on his arms until he leaned over her. His mouth made a mean-dering path from her throat to her collarbone and down to one taut nipple. She clutched at his broad back, digging her fingers into his skin and arching her back as he teased and tormented.

She traced the waistband of his pajama bottoms, pulling at the drawstring as they kissed repeatedly. He reached down and caught her hand when she tried to slip it inside his pants.

"Patience," he said.

"Nope," she said. "I'm done with slow and patient, aren't you?"

He hesitated, and she grinned at him before sliding her

hand into his pants and wrapping her fingers around his thickness. He groaned, his hips bucking against her, and a smug smile crossed her face as he stroked him firmly.

He kissed her hard and mapped each bump of her ribs with his fingers. He circled her belly button, and when he reached the waistband of her shorts and stopped, teasing the skin just above them, she grabbed his wrist and shoved his hand under her shorts.

He laughed against her lips, and she gave his bottom one a sharp nip that made him groan. "Touch me, Elias."

"Whatever you want, honey," he said.

He cupped her warmth, immediately driving her crazy with need as he circled and stroked and rubbed. She released him and clasped his naked back again, her breath puffing out of her in harsh pants. Shamefully, she was already close, and she moaned in protest when he stopped touching her.

His hands tugged at her shorts, and she lifted her hips. He swept them down her legs and tossed them on the floor before studying her naked body in the dim light of the Christmas lights.

"You're so beautiful, Ivy," he said hoarsely.

"So are you." She tugged at his pajama bottoms, and he removed them, dropping them over the side of the bed to join her pajamas. She studied his naked body, the broad chest and narrow hips, the thin line of hair that arrowed down from his belly button to the best Christmas present she could imagine.

"I need you," she whispered.

He reached across and grabbed a condom from the bedside table, opening it and rolling it on as her hands roamed across his shoulders and chest. She parted her legs, urging him between them with sharp tugs on his arms.

He stretched out between her legs, propping himself up

on his forearms above her, as the head of him pressed against her entrance.

"Still good?" he rasped.

"God, yes," she said. "Hurry, Elias."

He pushed into her, and they both moaned. He rested his forehead against hers and dropped a kiss against her mouth. "You feel so good, Ivy."

She slid her arms around his waist and rolled her hips against him, encouraging him to move. He groaned and thrust slowly and lightly. She met each thrust, and they found their rhythm quickly, their bodies moving as one.

Ivy clung to Elias, pleasure drenching her body as he brought her closer and closer to the edge with every thick slide and retreat, every kiss, every gentle caress. When he reached between them and rubbed her swollen clit, she muffled her cry of pleasure in his thick neck as her climax rushed over her in a relentless wave of ecstasy.

Her body quivering, she stroked Elias's back as his thrusts turned hard and quick. She met each one, watching his face in fascination as he grew close to his own release. He pushed in deep and threw his head back, the loud groan escaping his throat had her clapping her hand over his mouth to dampen the sound.

His big body shaking, he collapsed against her, his hot breath ruffling her hair as he fought to catch his breath. She hugged him tight. He was heavy, but she liked the weight of him on top of her. When he finally rolled off of her, she felt a pang of loss that she masked with a soft smile.

"Oh my God, Ivy." He disposed of the condom in the trash can next to the bed before pulling her into his embrace. She rested her cheek on his chest, listening to the heavy beat of his heart. "That was amazing."

"Hmm," she said. "It really was."

He stroked her back with long sweeps of his fingers. They stayed silent as their breathing returned to normal. Ivy was already feeling sleepy, and she snuggled closer as Elias smoothed her hair back from her face.

"Ivy?"

"Hmm?" she mumbled.

"Merry Christmas."

She smiled as her eyes drifted closed. "Merry Christmas, Elias."

CHAPTER 11

"Wait," Bryce, her lap covered by two feral cats, and her body sandwiched between two of the rescue dogs, leaned forward on the bed, "you're telling me that you and Elias had sex on Christmas Eve and that was it. You didn't sleep together again the next night?"

"Um… yes." Ivy bunched the blanket around her and looked away. It was close to midnight, and despite how tired she was, she hadn't objected when Bryce showed up at her bedroom door with two mugs of hot chocolate and the desire to chat.

"Ivy," Bryce said, "you have that look on your face."

"What look?"

"The one that says I am lying through my teeth."

"Fine!" she said. "We had sex again on Christmas Day. But, c'mon, we had to share the bed again, and it was cold in the house, and it's a proven fact that sex warms up a person."

"Oh, right, of course." Bryce laughed so loudly that the two cats hissed and took off from her lap, diving under the bed. "You had to have sex for warmth purposes. Makes total sense. So, Elias's parents can't afford to heat their house, is what you're saying."

Ivy scowled at her. "Keep your voice down. I don't want Nana knowing that Elias and I slept together."

"Why not?" Bryce lowered her voice.

"Because it was a casual thing and I don't want Nana thinking badly of me," Ivy said.

"Please, she has a casual thing with the Widow Smith, remember?" Bryce said.

Ivy just shrugged before reaching out and running her fingers through the thick fur of the dog crowded up against her. Tucker was a young and friendly husky cross, and he immediately rolled onto his back, his tongue lolling from his mouth. She rubbed his belly as Bryce said, "So, you had sex twice with Elias."

"Three times," Ivy said, her face reddening. "We had sex this morning before we joined his family for breakfast."

Bryce grinned at her. "How was sex with the handsome Dr. Hart?"

"Amazing," Ivy admitted. "He's very, um, good at sex-related things."

Bryce burst into laughter, quelling the sound by tucking her face into the crook of her elbow. "Oh my God, Ivy, what is going on with you? Normally, you're happy to spill the details."

Ivy didn't reply. What happened between her and Elias felt special and weirdly intimate in a way that sex with her previous boyfriends had not, and sharing her usual details with Bryce didn't seem right to her.

He isn't your boyfriend.

She swallowed hard. No, he wasn't. He was her boss, and that was it. What happened over Christmas was finished, and she needed to accept that and move on. It'd been her idea after all.

"You okay, honey?" Bryce squeezed her knee.

"Yes," Ivy took a sip of her hot chocolate. "Just fine."

"You're really not going to keep seeing Elias?"

"No. I told you, this was just a casual thing that we both agreed would end as soon as we left his parents' place. We left this afternoon, it's over."

"You're okay with that?"

"Yes," she lied. "Perfectly fine."

It was obvious that Bryce didn't believe her, but Ivy was relieved when she changed the subject. "How did the visit with his family go?"

"Really well. His mom and dad were so nice and made me feel welcome, and his grandma is a sweetheart. His parents donated to the rescue as a Christmas present to me, and NeeNee had knitted me a scarf." Ivy glanced at the scarf on her nightstand. "They were just… really lovely."

"Why do you look so sad about that?" Bryce asked.

Ivy combed some loose fur from Tucker's coat with her fingers. "I feel bad about lying to them. They were nice and so happy, especially NeeNee, about our engagement. I think they might be really upset when we," she made quotation marks with her fingers, "break up in January. And I already told Elias to tell his family that it's me who breaks up with him, but now that I've met them, I hate that they'll hate me for breaking it off with Elias."

"Do you regret helping him?" Bryce said.

"No, maybe… I don't know," Ivy said. "I mean, it worked out well for the rescue, and it did help him get out of a tough spot, but…"

"But now you're in love with him and super sad," Bryce said.

Ivy blinked at her. "I'm not in love with Elias."

Bryce slid off the bed and patted her leg. Two of the three dogs jumped off the bed, but Tucker stayed where he was, his face buried in the quilt and soft snores reverberating from his body.

"Good night, honey," Bryce said as she and the dogs headed toward the door.

"Bryce, I'm not in love with Elias," Ivy repeated.

Bryce paused in the doorway and pointed at Ivy's hand. "Just make sure you take off your engagement ring before you go to the clinic tomorrow."

Ivy's mouth dropped open, and she stared at the ring on her finger as Bryce left her bedroom. She'd completely forgotten to return it to Elias, and he hadn't asked her for it back.

Because he wants you to have it. He loves you, too, Ivy.

She shook her head and reached for the ring. He didn't love her. He'd forgotten about the ring, just like she had. Nothing more.

She paused with the ring halfway off her finger before pushing it back on, shutting off the light, and snuggling under the covers. It wouldn't hurt to wear the ring until tomorrow before she left for work.

———

ELIAS STARED BLANKLY AT HIS COMPUTER SCREEN. WHAT WAS he doing again? He studied the screen for another thirty seconds before remembering. Right. Entering the health notes for the guinea pig he'd just examined.

He tapped at the keyboard, finished the notes, and then exited the program, leaning back in his office chair. He scrubbed a hand across his face. He hadn't shaved this morning, and he knew he had dark circles under his eyes. It was what happened when he got barely two hours of sleep.

He swivelled in his chair and looked out the window at the falling snow. It shouldn't have been so difficult to sleep alone after only three nights of sharing a bed with Ivy, but he'd tossed and turned in his suddenly too-big bed for hours last night.

He leaned forward, resting his elbows on his knees and staving off the urge to ask Ivy to come to his office. What exactly would he say to her? They'd agreed to go back to friends only after Christmas, and last night when he'd driven her home, she hadn't made any indication she wanted something different.

It was for the best. A relationship with an employee was asking for trouble. Only... it suddenly felt like being with Ivy was worth the risk. He missed her.

She was here in the clinic, and she'd been her usual friendly self to him from the minute he arrived, but he still missed her. He didn't think he imagined that she was subtly attempting to keep her distance from him. He missed her soft laugh, sweet scent, and the way she smiled when he held her hand.

He groaned and turned his chair around to face his desk again. He was acting like a love-struck fool, and it was annoying as hell. Just because he and Ivy got along well, had great chemistry, and she was unbelievable in bed didn't mean they should date.

That's exactly what it means, idiot.

"Elias?"

He glanced up, his heart doing that skip-a-beat thing when he saw Ivy standing in the doorway. "Ivy, hi. Hey, uh, how are you?"

"Good. Do you have a minute?"

He nodded. "Yeah, my next client isn't here yet."

She glanced behind her before shutting his office door. She approached his desk, her manner like a skittish bunny, and he stayed perfectly still as she stopped in front of his desk. "I wanted to give this back to you."

She reached into the shirt pocket of her scrubs and set the ring on the desk in front of him. He stared at it, a weird tingle of dismay starting in the pit of his stomach, before he scooped it up and tucked it into the top drawer of his desk. "Thank you."

"I'm sorry I forgot to give it back yesterday," she said.

"That's okay, I forgot to ask for it." He hadn't thought of it at all. But now, staring at the empty space on her ring finger where the ring once sat made him feel irritated and annoyed. "Is that everything?"

The tentative smile dropped from her face at his cold tone, and she nodded. "That's it."

Shit! He was being a total jackass to Ivy, and she didn't deserve that. He searched desperately for something to say as she opened the door. "Ivy!"

"Yeah?" She paused in the doorway but didn't turn around.

Think, man, think!

"Um... feral cats!" His mouth spat out the words, and his brain cheered.

"I'm sorry?" She turned around slowly.

"The feral cats you wanted me to take. When would you like me to pick them up?" He clenched his hands into fists under the desk. Not that he wanted to be scooping litter boxes on a daily basis, but if it meant the chance to spend a few extra minutes with Ivy, it was worth it.

"Oh," she said. "You know, you don't have to do that. You've already done so much and -"

"I want to," he said quickly. "A deal's a deal, right?"

"Right," she said. She chewed on her bottom lip. "Um, I could bring them by to your place tonight, say around seven? If that works for you?"

"Sure," he said. "That works perfectly. I'll prep the spare room for them."

"Okay," she said. "The rescue provides all the supplies, so I'll bring those with me."

"Perfect. I'll see you at seven." His voice was too loud, and he cleared his throat as Whitney stopped in front of his office.

"Dr. Hart? Your next appointment is here."

"Thanks, Whitney. Be right there."

Whitney turned to Ivy. "Millie is under and ready for her dental."

"Okay." Ivy aimed another uncertain smile his way before following Whitney.

Elias leaned back in his chair, excitement brewing in his belly. Ivy was coming by his place tonight. Sure, nothing would happen, but just having her at his place made his irritation disappear and happiness take its place.

ELIAS SQUATTED AND STARED AT THE CATS HIDING UNDER THE bed. "How long until they come out from under the bed, do you think?"

"Probably not as long as you might think." Ivy finished adding litter to the box and set it in the corner. The food and water dishes were set up in the other corner, and she placed a large grocery bag containing both wet and dry food near them. "Morty and Mahi are only semi-feral. Plus, they're used to dogs, so Bella shouldn't bother them too much when they do decide to come out and explore."

"Okay." He studied the baby gate that Ivy had brought with her. "What's with the baby gate?"

"Once the cats are more comfortable and ready to explore the rest of the house, you can use the baby gate across the doorway to keep Bella from eating their food and," she made a face, "raiding their litter box for poop treats."

He laughed. "Smart thinking."

"Keep them in the room for a day or two, though, all right? Let them get used to their new space before you give them too much freedom."

"I will," he said as he followed her out of the spare room and down the hallway. His place was a small bungalow, and he freed Bella from his bedroom as they passed by. She immediately ran to the guest room, sniffing at the bottom of the door.

Ivy was already headed toward the front door, and he said, "Would you like a drink?"

She hesitated before saying, "Sure."

She followed him into the kitchen, studying the small space with its white cabinets, stainless steel appliances, and light blue walls. "This is nice."

"Thanks." He opened the fridge. "I have beer, juice, or water. Or I could make you some hot chocolate."

She smiled nervously. "Hot chocolate would be good."

"Have a seat." He pointed to the small table, and Ivy sat down as he popped the hot chocolate pod into the coffee machine and set a mug under it. As it poured, he stared out the window above the sink. "It's really coming down out there."

Ivy nodded. "The roads were already a bit slippery when I drove here."

He set the mug of hot chocolate in front of her and sat down, watching as she took a sip.

"It's good, thank you," she said.

"You're welcome." He studied her sweet face. She looked a little tired, and he wondered if she'd had trouble sleeping last night like he did.

"I'm sorry I kept the ring an extra night," she said abruptly. "I didn't mean to do that."

"I know. It's not a big deal," he said.

"Thanks again for taking the cats," she said.

"No problem."

As she sipped at her hot chocolate, he cast about for something else to say. The problem was, he couldn't think of anything to say other than how much he missed her, how much he wanted her in his bed again.

As the seconds ticked by and the silence grew big and uncomfortable, he could feel his own anxiety rising. Shit, if he didn't say something, she'd leave.

As if she read his thoughts, she stood up and carried her half-full mug to the sink, dumping it down the drain and rinsing it out. "Sorry," she said, "but I should probably go before the roads get worse. I'm not the most confident driver, and I hate driving in the snow so -"

"Maybe you should stay the night," he said.

She stared up at him as he joined her at the sink. "What?"

"It's snowing pretty heavily. It's probably safer for you to stay the night with me rather than risk driving."

He could see a small smile playing on her lips, and he reached out and tugged her against him. He put his arms around her waist as she rested her hands on his forearms. "Safer, huh?"

"Yes." He bent down and kissed the sensitive spot behind her ear. "I would feel terrible if something happened to you while you were driving home. Best not to take the risk."

"That's very thoughtful of you," she said.

"I'm a thoughtful guy." He kissed down her neck, loving the soft moan she made when he cupped her breast.

"You are, and you do have that empty guest room right down the hall."

He growled at her, and she giggled when he picked her up. She wrapped her legs around his waist and kissed him as he walked down the hallway toward his bedroom. Bella was still sniffing at the guest room door, and she gave them a brief disinterested look before lying down with her nose pressed against the space at the bottom of the door.

"Looks like Bella's got the door blocked," he said. "I guess you'll have to share my room with me."

"Bad Bella," Ivy said before nipping at his neck.

"I don't know," he said, setting her on her feet in his bedroom and reaching for the buttons on her shirt. "I'm leaning toward 'good Bella' myself."

Ivy laughed as she pulled his shirt up and over his head and then reached for the button on his jeans. "I assume you're going to give her a good treat for being your wingman?"

"A bone *and* a whole box of biscuits." He tugged her shirt off and unclasped her bra, dropping them both on the floor.

He cupped her breasts, groaning when she reached inside his pants and wrapped her fingers around him. "God, Ivy, that feels so good."

She kissed his chest, and when her tongue flicked at his flat nipple, he groaned again and cupped the back of her head, threading his fingers through her silky, soft hair. Her warm kisses and the way her hand stroked him so perfectly had every one of his nerve endings zinging.

"Naked, now," he said hoarsely as he tugged her hand free.

She wiggled out of her jeans and panties as he stripped off the rest of his clothes. She giggled when he nearly fell over trying to remove his socks and then made a soft squeal of surprise when he picked her up and tossed her onto his bed. Laughing, she bounced to a stop, and he kissed her shin before peeling both her socks off.

"Thank you," she said.

"You're welcome." He nudged her legs apart and kissed his way up her smooth shin before nipping at her inner thigh. He settled on the bed between her legs, his broad shoulders pushing her thighs even further apart.

"Elias?" Ivy's voice was breathless, and she moaned when he pressed a kiss against the soft curls at the top of her sex.

"Yes, Ivy?" He tasted her sweetness with a long, slow lick before raising his head. "What is it you were going to say?"

She gave him a dazed look of incomprehension as her fingers curled into his hair. "I... I forget."

He kissed her inner thigh before burying his face between her thighs. He licked and sucked and teased until Ivy was grinding her pelvis against him and the room was filled with the sweet sounds of her pleasure as she climaxed.

Her body shuddering, she collapsed against the bed, her chest heaving for air, and her hands clenched tightly in the sheets. He grabbed a condom from the nightstand and rolled it on before easing between her open thighs.

"Ready?" He nuzzled her throat and placed a kiss against one stiff nipple.

"Yes," she gasped out, her hands curling around his waist as she hooked her legs around his thighs. She rested her feet on the back of his thighs, her fingers digging into his hips as he entered her fully with one hard push.

She was warm and wet and so tight. He gritted his teeth

against the urge to move hard and fast and instead made a few slow thrusts. They both moaned, and Ivy squeezed his waist and pressed a kiss against his mouth, her tongue teasing his bottom lip.

"Harder," she demanded.

He moved harder and faster, their breaths mingling and their bodies moving together in a quickening rhythm that had him on the edge of his orgasm. He pushed deeper, kissing Ivy hard on the mouth, their tongues tangling together as his climax roared over him. He released her mouth and shouted her name like a prayer as his thrusts slowed.

Panting, he rested his forehead against hers, smiling when she traced circles on his back and said, "You good?"

"Incredible," he said. He wanted to stay where he was forever, but he forced himself to move away from her. He slid out of bed and went to the primary bathroom, tossing the condom before returning to the bedroom.

Ivy was standing in the middle of the room with her panties on and her bra in her hands, and he scowled at her. "What are you doing?"

"It's late," she said. "I should go."

"It's only nine. Stay," he said. "Please."

She paused, the look on her face wavering between pleased and indecisive. "Are you sure?"

"Positive," he said. "I want you to stay the night with me."

"I'll need to leave early in the morning," she said.

"I'll set my alarm. Even make you your coffee before you go." He gave her what he hoped was his most charming smile. "Stay, Ivy."

"All right." She climbed back into bed, and his face nearly split in half by his grin, he climbed in next to her and spooned her.

"Are you hungry or thirsty?" he asked. "I could grab my tablet and we could watch something on Netflix."

She shook her head, wiggling herself back against him until the entire lengths of their bodies were touching. She yawned and rested her head on the pillow. "Do you mind if we just relax? I'm exhausted. I slept terribly last night."

He pressed a kiss against the back of her shoulder and rested his head on the pillow behind hers. "I didn't sleep well either."

"No?" Her fingers traced along his forearm.

"No. I missed having you in my bed."

"I missed being in your bed," she admitted.

He kissed her shoulder again, and she sighed. "So much for keeping our distance once we returned home, huh? We probably shouldn't do this again, Elias."

"I know," he said. "Go to sleep, honey."

She lifted his hand to her mouth and kissed his knuckles. "Good night, Elias."

CHAPTER 12

"Good morning, dear heart."

Ivy screamed and dropped her purse on the hallway floor. Nana leaned against the door jamb of the kitchen and grinned at her. "Ivy, hush. You'll wake Bryce, and you know she isn't a morning person."

"You almost gave me a heart attack, Nana!" Her heart racing, Ivy rescued her purse from the floor before Zoe could carry it off. "What are you doing up? It's not even six."

"Oh, I don't seem to sleep as well as I used to in my youth," Nana said. "Come have a coffee with me, dearest."

Ivy followed her into the kitchen, sinking into the chair and sipping gratefully at the coffee Nana set in front of her. She'd already had one cup of coffee at Elias's this morning, but he'd also woken her up twice in the middle of the night to have sex, and she was still tired despite how well she'd slept in his bed.

She wasn't upset about him waking her up. It was their last night together, and being with him was more important to her than sleep.

It doesn't have to be your last night with him.

"Dearest?"

"Sorry, what?" Ivy glanced at her grandmother.

"I asked how your night was." Nana petted Zoe, who was leaning against her legs, and then gave Ivy a delicate look.

"Oh, um, it was good." Her plan to slip into the house and pretend that she'd just gotten home really late last night ended the moment Nana said good morning.

"How is Elias?"

"Oh, I wasn't with Elias, I was, uh…"

Her tired brain couldn't think up an excuse fast enough.

Nana laughed. "Dearest, I might be old, but my brain isn't addled yet. You went to Elias's last night to drop off Morti and Mahi and never returned."

"I'm sorry I didn't text," Ivy said.

Nana waved her off. "You're a grown woman. You aren't required to text me when you have overnight plans with a man."

Ivy groaned and took a big gulp of the hot coffee, scalding her tongue. "Nana, it isn't, I mean, what we're doing is not…"

Nana set her coffee cup down. "I assume what you're trying to say is that you and Elias have a relationship much like the Widow Smith and I do. Is that right?"

"Yeah," she said.

Nana cocked her head at her. "Well, you know that there isn't anything wrong with that, but you look so miserable that it makes me wonder if this type of relationship is the right one for you, sweetheart."

"It is… it has to be," she said. "Besides, it doesn't matter. We agreed it was just a temporary thing over the Christmas holidays, and now it's over. Last night was an… accident."

"I do hate it when I accidentally fall onto a penis," Nana said as Bryce, followed by Tucker and the rest of the foster dogs, walked into the kitchen.

Bryce stumbled to a stop, staring blearily at Nana and Ivy. "Who fell onto a penis?"

"Ivy did, dear," Nana said before standing. "Would you like a cup of coffee?"

HE WAS BEING RIDICULOUS.

Elias drove his car toward Ivy's house, telling himself he was taking this route because it was a shortcut home, not because he was hoping to catch her on the porch so he could casually say hello.

It's after nine o'clock on a Thursday night and there's a bad snowstorm happening, but yeah, Ivy might be just hanging out on her front porch and will see you driving by, flag you down, and invite you in for sex. Solid plan, idiot.

Okay, so maybe it was a stupid plan, but he was driving himself crazy sitting at home. He'd left the house half an hour ago with no actual plan of what to do, just knowing that he couldn't sit there a minute longer in the silence.

He turned down Ivy's street, the rhythmic squeal of the wipers as they strained to clear the snow from the windshield making him clench his teeth in irritation.

He'd seen Ivy all day at work, but she'd been almost painfully formal with him, just like she'd been since she left his place early Wednesday morning. She said they really couldn't do this anymore, and the last two days had made it obvious that she meant it, so what exactly was he doing? He needed to respect her desire for a friendship only. Driving by her house late at night just in the hopes that he might catch a glimpse –

He slammed on the brakes, the car skidding in the fresh snow as he stared at Ivy's house. Holy shit, she *was* on the front porch. Bryce was with her, and they were both staring suspiciously at a large cardboard box sitting on the porch. He pulled into her driveway and climbed out of the car, hurrying up the slippery front walk toward them.

"Elias? What are you doing here?" Ivy said.

"I was just, uh, driving by and saw you on the porch." He joined them, shoving his hands deep into his pockets. The wind blew the soft flakes of snow into his face as Bryce grinned at him.

"Just happened to be driving by, huh?"

If his face got any warmer, the snowflakes would melt the instant they touched it. "Uh, yeah. What's in the box?"

"We don't know," Ivy said. She was wearing that hideously hairy robe again, but this time she had a jacket over it with snow boots on her feet and a toque jammed onto her head. "We were just about to open it."

"I told you to call me when this happened again," he said.

She just shrugged, and when he crouched beside the box, Bryce backed up a few steps. "Please don't let it be another snake," she mumbled.

The box was closed with duct tape, and he peeled it back before opening the flaps. It was full of newspapers, and he glanced up at Ivy. "Do you have any gloves? I don't want to stick my bare hand in there without – shit!"

The puppy burst out of the box like it was on a spring. Crying and whimpering, it scrambled up the front of his chest, licking frantically at his face and hands as its tiny body shivered wildly.

"Oh, sweet baby," Bryce said. "Poor little thing." She took the puppy from Elias just as a second puppy cautiously poked its head out of the newspaper. It stared at Elias, and he scooped it out of the box and handed it to Ivy before poking around in the paper for more. The box was empty, and he straightened.

"Just the two," he said.

"Okay, thank you, Elias. We'll take it from here," Ivy said. She smiled awkwardly at him and opened the door. "Uh, good night."

"Maybe you should come in and do exams of the puppies," Bryce said. "Since you're already here. Do you mind, Elias?"

He could have kissed her with gratitude. "Not at all."

"Perfect. Come on in," Bryce said.

He followed them into the house, removing his jacket and boots before joining them in the kitchen. Bryce handed her puppy to him. "Thanks again, Elias. Good night."

"Where are you going?" Ivy said. She had tossed her robe and toque on one of the chairs, and she was wearing the same pajamas she'd worn at his parents' place. Hot memories flooded his brain, and he looked away from her immediately, praying he didn't get a damn erection.

"To bed. I have the worst headache," Bryce said. "Killing me. Can't stay on my feet a minute longer."

"I need help with the puppies," Ivy said with a pointed glare.

"I need to take care of the other dogs," Bryce said.

"They're sleeping in your room," Ivy said.

"Elias can help you. Right, Elias?" Bryce said.

"Yes," he said.

"I'm sure he has better things to do than help me with puppies," Ivy said.

Bryce smiled at him. "Do you have other plans tonight, Elias?"

"I do not," he said. Ivy's best friend was the best wingman ever.

"See. He doesn't have plans," Bryce said to Ivy. "Good night, you two."

She left the kitchen, and Ivy sighed and shook her head. "Could she have been any more obvious?"

Elias laughed. "I really like Bryce."

"These guys look about eight weeks, yeah?" Ivy said.

He nodded, and she handed him the second puppy. "I'll hunt down a pen to put them in while you examine them."

Ivy returned just as he finished his examination. The puppies were much warmer and wigglier, and Ivy set up a baby gate across the doorway of the kitchen. "Go ahead and put them down."

He set them on the floor, and they explored cautiously as Ivy pulled out a can of puppy food from the pantry.

"I thought you were closed to intakes," he said.

"We are." He could see the stress and worry embedded in her face. "But I can't leave them out in the cold to die either. Shit, the rescue only has a few cans of puppy food left." She rubbed at her forehead. "Tomorrow I'll put a call out for donations of puppy food on the Facebook page, but seeing as it's just after Christmas, I'm doubtful we'll get much interest or donations."

There was a low growl from the doorway. He turned to see a large black and white cat sitting on top of the baby gate and staring menacingly at the puppies.

"Be nice, Winston," Ivy said.

The cat growled again, and Ivy brandished a food-covered spoon at him. "Go on then. There are plenty of other spots in the house that don't have puppies in them."

The cat leaped down from the gate and stalked down the hall with its tail held high in the air. Ivy rolled her eyes. "He's such a weird cat. Hates the dogs but can't stay away from them either. Do the puppies seem healthy?"

"Yes. They look like Boston terrier crosses. The bigger one," he pointed to the brown and white puppy who was now pulling at his pant leg with its needle-sharp teeth, "is a boy. And the little black and white one is a girl."

The girl joined her brother in pulling on Elias's pant leg, and he reached down and picked them both up. They licked his face with their warm, wet tongues as the scent of puppy breath washed over him. "They're sweet little things."

"The terriers always are," Ivy said. She set two dishes of food down on the floor, and Elias brought the babies over and set them in front of the food. They immediately buried their faces in the food, chewing enthusiastically as they smeared wet food all over their faces.

Ivy laughed, and some of the worry in Elias's chest eased. He hated seeing her look so tired and defeated. He reached out and took her hand. "It'll be all right, honey. I'll pick up some puppy food tomorrow before I come into the clinic. Bring the puppies in with you, and we'll do the first vaccinations and deworming. All right?"

She stared at their clasped hands. "You don't have to buy food for the rescue, Elias."

"I want to," he said.

Her smile was a bit cheeky. "I don't suppose you'd like to foster the babies, huh?"

He laughed. "As much as Bella would love that, I'm gonna have to pass. Puppies are way too much work, and also, I'm pretty sure my cats wouldn't like it."

Her smile widened. "Your cats?"

He shrugged. "They're coming out of their shells surprisingly quickly. They showed up in my bedroom last night. Slept on the bed and everything for a while."

"That's good," she said.

They watched in silence as the puppies finished eating.

Ivy wiped their faces and paws clean and gave the puppies to him as she cleaned up the mess they'd made on the floor.

Warm with full bellies, the puppies fell asleep almost immediately. Still carrying them, Elias followed Ivy down the hall. "Where's your grandmother?"

"Well, I thought it was her bridge night with Mrs. Jorgen's, but found out recently that she's actually having a secret romance with the Widow Smith. She's at his place tonight."

He stumbled to a stop. "What? Isn't he like eighty-five years old?"

"Yep," Ivy said.

"But he has a bad hip," Elias said. "He tells me about it every time he brings Juniper in for her annual."

"Nana rides him, apparently." Ivy opened the door to their right. "Bring the puppies in here."

He followed her into the room, stopping short when he saw the bed. It had an old-fashioned steel headboard and footboard with a colourful quilt and three cats covering the mattress. They all hissed and jumped off the bed, slinking out of the room with angry looks his way.

"Is this, uh, your room?" he asked.

She nodded, and he could feel sweat breaking out on his back. He was in Ivy's room, standing near Ivy's bed. The bed that she slept in every night. Maybe naked.

"Elias?" Ivy was staring at him.

He really needed to get it together and stop acting like a horny teenage boy. "Sorry."

He carried the puppies to where she was standing next to one of those foldable metal dog pens. She'd covered the floor with puppy pee pads, and there were a few blankets arranged into a cozy bed in the corner of the pen.

He eased the puppies down onto the blanket and stepped

out of the pen. Ivy closed it up and secured it before smiling at him. "Thank you."

"You're welcome." He studied her mouth before looking away. "I guess I should go. It's getting late, and the roads are bad."

She didn't reply. Disappointment coating his stomach, he headed toward her bedroom door.

"Elias?"

He turned around. "Yeah?"

"Maybe you should stay."

He studied her in the dim light of the nightstand lamp. "Is that what you really want?"

"The roads are pretty bad," she said with a soft smile. "It's not safe for you to drive."

He shrugged, a smile curving up his lips. "They're pretty slippery. But if you don't want -"

"I want," she said. Her voice was low and needy. "Please stay."

He shut the bedroom door and crossed the room to pull her into his arms. "I've missed you."

He buried his face in her hair as she giggled. "You see me every day."

"I know." He pressed a kiss against her jaw. "I still miss you."

"I miss you too." She stared up at him. "I'm glad you're staying."

"I'm glad you asked." He picked her up, making her giggle again, and carried her to the bed. He laid her down on it before covering her body with his and kissing her sweet mouth. "You're positive you want me to stay, Ivy?"

She cupped his face and gave him a lingering kiss that sent his pulse into a jittery beat. "I've never been more certain of anything in my life, Elias."

———

THE BUZZ OF HIS CELL PHONE PULLED ELIAS FROM SLEEP. HE reached for it blearily, squinting at the screen before answering. "Hello?"

Ivy was a warm, soft lump pressed against his back, and he closed his eyes, listening as the caller spoke frantically. When they stopped to take in a breath, he said, "Okay. I'll be at the clinic in fifteen minutes. Meet me there."

He disconnected the call and checked the time. It was just after five in the morning, and he groaned inwardly. The last thing he wanted to do was leave Ivy's warm bed, but as the only vet clinic in their small town, he was technically an emergency clinic as well.

"Who that?" Ivy mumbled into his back as her arm tightened around his waist.

"Patricia Mullens," he said. "Her cat ate part of her poinsettia."

"Uh oh," Ivy muttered.

"I have to go." He patted her hand. "Let me go, honey."

"Need me to go with?" She kissed his back and patted his hip.

"No, stay in bed. I'll see you at the clinic in a couple of hours."

She yawned and snuggled deeper under the quilt as he slid out of the bed. His fingers and toes turned cold almost immediately, and he stared longingly at Ivy and her warm bed before leaning over and pressing a kiss against her mouth. "Bye, Ivy."

"Bye, honey," she mumbled. "Be careful driving."

"I will." He dressed quickly and quietly, then tiptoed past the puppies who, miraculously, had slept through the night.

He stepped out into the hallway, easing the door shut

behind him. He caught movement to his left and froze, staring in shock at the old man quietly closing the door of a room further down the hall.

They stared silently at each other for almost a minute. The older man's thin hair was sticking up from his scalp like porcupine quills, and he held a cane in one hand. He smoothed his hair down with a trembling hand and gave Elias an oddly dignified nod.

"Dr. Hart."

"Widow Smith."

CHAPTER 13

"Are you kidding me? Elias ran into the Widow Smith in the hall this morning?" Bryce's laughter pealed out.

Ivy glanced around the grocery store. She was on her phone with Bryce, but voices carried on cell phones. "Keep it down, Bryce. I'm at the store picking up some snacks for the clinic, and people are gonna hear you through the phone."

"Sorry!" Bryce lowered her voice. "That's hilarious, though, you have to admit it."

Ivy added bananas to her basket. "It really is. After Elias told me, I texted Nana during my break, and she said the roads were so bad that when the Widow Smith picked her up from Mrs. Jorgen's, they came back to our place because it was closer."

"I can't believe both you and your grandmother had men sneaking out at the same time," Bryce said with another giggle. "Also, why is everyone in the house getting laid except me? How is that fair?"

"He wasn't sneaking out." Ivy glanced around and lowered her voice. "He had an emergency call."

"So, are you two officially a couple yet, or what?" Bryce asked.

"I don't know," Ivy admitted. "We keep telling each other that we can't sleep together again, but then…"

"You bang again," Bryce said.

"Yeah."

Bryce's tone turned somber. "All kidding aside, Ivy, you should date him. I know you're worried about your job and about the rescue, but Elias is a good guy. He won't do what Ray did."

"I thought Ray was a good guy too, remember?" Ivy said.

"I know. He fooled all of us, though," Bryce said. "You can't keep beating yourself up over that. You made a mistake. So, what? It's in the past."

"Yeah, but this mistake is still putting the rescue in jeopardy," Ivy said. "Without Ray's father's yearly donation, I'm not sure how much longer we can keep going with the rescue if we don't figure out this fundraising thing."

"I'm working on it," Bryce said. "I might have a couple of people interested in volunteering for the position."

"Seriously?" Some of the tension in Ivy's shoulders eased. "That would be awesome."

"I'll let you know," Bryce said. "Oh, and did Andrea text you about the puppies?"

"Yes, and she stopped by the clinic earlier this morning and picked up the two puppies. Thank God."

"She's a good egg," Bryce said. "All I said to her was that we had two puppies dropped off last night, and she immediately said she would foster them. Hey, what are your plans for New Year's?"

"I'm not sure," Ivy said. "I didn't have anything planned but maybe…"

"Maybe you'll be spending the evening with a handsome vet?" Bryce teased.

"Maybe. Listen, I have to run. Elias sent me out to restock the clinic snack drawer, not gab on the phone to you."

"Later, babe." Bryce ended the call, and Ivy stuck her phone back into her pocket. Bryce was right, Elias wasn't like Ray, and it was time she stopped living in the past and –

Not looking where she was going, Ivy ran into the broad back of a man standing near the apples.

"Oh, I'm so sorry. Please excuse me. I didn't..."

Her voice died in her throat, and her stomach immediately felt like it had a heavy, hot rock sitting in it. She stared mutely at the silver-haired man as he gazed down at her with barely disguised loathing.

She wanted to turn and run away. Instead, she straightened her spine and stared directly at Ray's father. "Excuse me, Mr. Dorchester, I didn't see you there."

"Still running the rescue, Ms. West?" His voice was icy cold.

He knew damn well she was, but she said, "I am."

"Surprising. I always thought it took a person with a heart to do that type of work. I guess I was wrong."

She gritted her teeth. Ray had lied to his father about why they broke up, just like he'd lied to everyone else in their small town.

Let it go, Ivy. It doesn't matter.

"Do you feel any remorse for what you've done, Ms. West?"

"I need to go," she said.

He shoved his hands into his jacket and said, "When the rescue closes because you're a foolish girl who broke my son's heart, are you even going to feel bad? Do you even care at all about those innocent animals, or do you treat them as callously as you treated my Ray?"

"Mr. Dorchester, what happened between Ray and me -"

"What happened is that you decided to break his heart. You decided that he wasn't good enough for you, and you were just," he leaned in, the smell of his cologne making her feel a little nauseous, "cocky enough to believe there wouldn't be consequences to your actions."

"Mr. Dorchester -"

"You think I don't know that the rescue is on the verge of collapse? It's a small town, Ms. West, and people talk. Your rescue is almost done, and all of those animals you keep saying you love so much? They'll be left out in the cold to starve, and it'll be your fault because you're a cold and selfish -"

Something inside of Ivy snapped like a guitar string strung too tight. "Ray cheated on me!"

Her hands clenched around the shopping basket handle in tight fists, she said, "I know you think your son is perfect, but he cheated on me. I broke up with him because I found him in bed with Cynthia Waters."

Ray's father took a step back, his face slack with surprise. "I... what did you say?"

"Your perfect child? The one who you think walks on damn water? He cheated on me with another woman, and do you know what he told me when I said it was over? He said if I told anyone what he'd done, he would make sure that you never donated to our rescue again."

She laughed bitterly. "I kept my mouth shut. I let Ray walk around town, telling anyone who would listen how cold and heartless Ivy had broken his heart. But it didn't matter, because you decided to stop donating anyway."

Her anger was starting to deflate, the familiar guilt and

misery scurrying in to take its place. "I let Ray paint me as the bad guy because the rescue matters to me, those animals. *matter* to me. I made a mistake dating your son. The money you so generously donated every year helped the rescue tremendously. So, yeah, dating someone who had the power to directly affect the rescue's ability to keep going was a terrible idea."

She took a deep breath, blinking back the hot tears that were threatening to fall. "Thank you, Mr. Dorchester. Seeing you today was a good reminder that I can never make that mistake again."

———

ELIAS STOOD JUST INSIDE HIS OFFICE DOORWAY. HIS LAST client had left ten minutes ago, and Joanna, the receptionist, had already left. Ivy and Whitney were in the back finishing with clean up, and he watched as Ivy cleaned one of the examining tables with disinfectant.

Something had upset her, but he didn't know what. She was fine all morning, acting her usual self, until she returned from the grocery store. She'd been quiet and withdrawn since then, and he was now weighing his earlier decision to talk to her after work about making their relationship official.

Do it. You love her, you know you do. She loves you, too.

He had no idea if she loved him or not, but until four hours ago, he was reasonably certain she would be willing to give dating a try. But the way she'd been avoiding him again this afternoon, he wasn't so sure.

"You ready to go, Ives?" Whitney asked.

"Just about. Give me two more minutes," Ivy said.

"Are you working tomorrow?" Whitney leaned against

the counter and watched as Ivy covered up the lab equipment.

"No." Ivy straightened the boxes of empty syringes on the counter. "I'm off until the clinic reopens on the third."

"Fun," Whitney said. "Any plans for New Year's?"

"Staying at home with my Nana, eating a shrimp ring, and watching the ball drop. You?"

Elias tamped down his hurt that Ivy wasn't even considering spending New Year's with him. Even if she was, it wasn't like she would tell Whitney she was.

"Yeah, a group of friends and I are having a party. It'll be fun. I'm glad Dr. Hart is closing the office early tomorrow. I still have to pick up the beer and champagne, and I'm exhausted tonight," Whitney said.

Ivy smiled at her. "Let me just get my jacket and then I'm ready to go."

"Ivy?" Elias stuck his head out of his office. "Do you have a minute?"

"Um, sure," Ivy said.

"Do you want me to wait for you?" Whitney asked.

"No, you go ahead. I'm sure it won't take long," Ivy said.

"It won't," Elias said. "Good night, Whitney."

"Good night, Dr. Hart." Whitney left, and Elias waited until he heard the front door close and lock before he walked toward Ivy.

She skittered back until her butt hit the counter. He stopped and said, "What's wrong?"

"Nothing," she replied. "Nothing's wrong."

"Something upset you while you were grocery shopping. Will you tell me what happened?"

She rubbed at her forehead, a telltale sign that she was upset. "Nothing happened. I, uh, have a bit of a headache. What did you need to talk to me about?"

He studied her for a moment. "Maybe we should talk about it later."

"No, it's fine." She smiled wanly at him and motioned for him to go on.

"Well, I've been thinking about us and where we go from here."

"Where we go from here," she repeated.

"Yes. My hesitation in dating you stemmed from my worry that you might quit on me if things didn't work out. You're my best vet tech, Ivy, and I don't want to lose you."

"You thought I would quit?" Her tone was one of skepticism.

"Yes. But I'm not worried about that anymore. I want to be with you, Ivy, and it's worth the risk to me that you might quit if we break up." He smiled at her. "I also should admit that I am one hundred percent confident it's going to work out for us."

She huffed out a disbelieving laugh. "I was worried that you would fire me if we broke up, and you're worried that I would quit. Elias, you know how much I need this job, right? You're the only vet clinic in town."

"I already told you I would never fire you because we stopped dating," he said. He pushed aside the hurt he felt that she still believed he would. "Ivy, I wouldn't do that."

She studied him, her face drawn and her eyes red like she was holding back tears. "Okay."

"I mean it," he said. "I need you at the clinic, Ivy. I'm not joking when I said you're the best vet tech I've ever worked with."

He thought that might make her feel better. Instead, the pinched look on her face grew, and she nodded before staring at the floor.

Feeling like something was going terribly wrong, but

unable to put his finger on the reason why, he put his arms around her and drew her in close. "This is a good thing, right? You know I would never fire you, and I know you won't quit, so we can try dating. I want to get to know you better, and I don't want to hide our relationship. Nothing is stopping us from -"

"There is," she said.

"What do you mean?"

Her face had gone pale, and this time he was certain she was struggling not to cry. "The rescue."

He stared at her in confusion. "The rescue? It's not a problem, honey. I know it's your priority and keeps you busy, and I understand. Hell, I'm busy with the clinic, right? So, we'll just have to make sure we carve out time for each other and -"

"It isn't that," she said.

"Then what is it?"

"If we break up," her voice was barely above a whisper, "and you stop helping us with the rescue, if you stop giving us a discount… the rescue is finished. We're barely making it as it is, and without your discount, we don't have a chance. I – we have a lot of animals in our care and I can't take that risk."

This time, it was impossible to push aside the hurt. Elias dropped his arms, stepping back and folding his arms across his chest. "Are you serious right now?"

"Elias -"

"No," he said as anger seeped in to overtake the hurt. "We've worked together for two years, Ivy. You've watched me burn the candle at both ends for months and months to help treat and save as many animals as I can, but you think I would abandon the rescue because you broke up with me?"

"Elias, I don't *want* to think that, but I have to be smart about this. The rescue relies on your discount, and if we don't have it -"

"Stop it," he said. "Stop acting like I'm some immature asshole who would intentionally destroy the rescue just to get back at you. That isn't me, and I can't believe you think it is."

"I'm sorry," she said.

"I am too," he said. "You should go. Forget what I said about dating. I think it's best if we go back to our previous working relationship only. I'm obviously not the person you thought I was, and you know what?" His smile felt thin and brittle on his face. "I'm really glad I'm not."

"DEAR HEART, PLEASE TELL US WHAT'S WRONG," NANA SAID softly.

Ivy threw a kernel of popcorn at Zoe. The dog caught it neatly in her mouth, and the other dogs all hurried over to sit at her feet. She threw each of them some popcorn before pulling the blanket up around her shoulders and staring blankly at the television screen. "Nothing's wrong."

"Bullshit," Bryce said. "You've been moping around the house since you got home from work last night."

"She's right," Nana said. She was sitting on the couch next to Bryce, and she patted her leg affectionately. "Dearest, pour me some more wine, would you?"

Bryce grabbed the wine bottle from the coffee table and poured more wine into Nana's glass.

"Thanks, sweetheart. Are you sure you don't want some? The Widow Smith gave it to me, and it's delicious."

"I'm sure," Bryce said. "Wine upsets my stomach. Ivy, maybe you should start drowning your sorrows in wine."

"I don't have any sorrows," Ivy said.

"Oh yeah? Because it's New Year's Eve and you're sitting at home in your pajamas with your Nana waiting to watch the ball drop on TV. I can't think of anything sadder. No offense, Nana," Bryce said.

"None taken, dearest." Nana patted her thigh again.

"You're here too," Ivy said moodily. "You're just as big a loser as I am."

"Touché," Bryce said with a grin.

Nana drank more wine. "She's right, sweetheart. You should be out celebrating with kids your own age. Even better, celebrate with Elias."

"Why would I do that?" Ivy said. "He's just my stupid boss, nothing more."

"Here we go," Bryce said. "Now we're getting to the real problem."

"There's no problem," Ivy snapped. "Just drop it, Bryce."

"Dear heart," Nana said.

Ivy stared at her lap, blinking back the tears fiercely. She wouldn't look at her Nana. Nope, she absolutely wouldn't look at her. Because if she did and she saw the sympathy in her Nana's gaze, she would lose it.

"Dearest, look at me," Nana said gently.

Ivy raised her gaze to her grandmother's and promptly burst into tears. Nana hopped off the couch, set her wine glass on the table, and hurried to Ivy. She sat down in the armchair with her, squeezing her narrow butt in beside Ivy's, and put her arms around her.

"Oh, sweet girl, tell me what's wrong."

"I screwed up, Nana," Ivy said before sniffing loudly. "I screwed up and now Elias hates me."

"I'm sure he doesn't hate you," Nana said. "Tell us what happened."

"HE MIGHT HATE YOU," BRYCE SAID FIFTEEN MINUTES LATER.

"Bryce!" Nana's look was fierce with disapproval, and Bryce wilted under her gaze.

"I'm sorry, Ivy, I didn't mean it to come out that way."

"It's okay." Ivy wiped at her cheeks with a tissue. "I know what I did, and I deserve for him to hate me. Seeing Ray's dad earlier, though, made me feel terrible and awful because he was right. The fact that the rescue is in trouble is my fault. When Elias said he wanted a relationship, I just kept thinking about what would happen if we broke up and…"

She blew her nose and stared miserably at Nana. "I hurt his feelings, Nana. I hurt him so much, and I can't stop thinking about the look on his face. I feel terrible for doing that to him, and I've texted him twice to say that I'm sorry, and he hasn't replied at all."

"Well, it did just happen last night, dearest," Nana said. "Maybe give the poor boy some time to process. I'm sure by the time you return to work, he'll be more willing to listen to your apology."

"Maybe," Ivy said. "But just thinking about going to work knowing that he hates me now…"

She buried her face in her hands. "I've messed things up so badly."

"Nothing is ever so messed up that it can't be fixed," Nana said. "Believe me. Give Elias a few days, then be honest with him about what happened with Ray. If he knew your past, then he'd have a better understanding of why you're so afraid."

"I don't want to tell him about Ray. I don't want him to see what an idiot I was and still am," Ivy said.

"A person is never an idiot for believing in the best of

someone, so stop that nonsense right now." Nana used her thumbs to wipe the tears from Ivy's cheeks. "I know you're sad and you feel guilty and you miss the man you love, but now's the time to buck up."

"Yeah, buck up," Bryce said.

Ivy and Nana glanced at her, and Bryce shrugged. "I'm not so good with the pep talks. Keep going, Nana."

"On Tuesday, you're going to go into work early and you're going to ask Elias to listen for five minutes to what you have to say," Nana said. "You're going to tell him all about Ray, you're going to admit that you love him, and you're going to ask for a second chance."

Ivy stared at her. "I don't know if I can do that."

Nana cupped her face, her hands warm and her eyes grave. "You can. Be brave, dear heart."

Ivy's phone rang, and Nana kissed her forehead before standing. "Best to answer that, dearest. It might be Elias."

Ivy snagged her phone from the folds of the blanket on her lap, studying the screen. "It isn't. Hello?"

She listened quietly, dismay growing in her belly, before nodding. "All right, I'll be right there. Apply pressure to the wound on his leg and cover him with a blanket to help keep him warm."

She disconnected the call and scrambled out of her chair.

"Who was that?" Bryce said.

"Joe McManus. He's got a badly injured stray dog that needs help. I have to go."

"I'm coming with you." Bryce jumped up off the couch and followed her out of the living room.

CHAPTER 14

"I vy, you have to call him," Bryce said from the back seat.

"I know." Ivy started the car. "What if he doesn't answer?"

"He will."

"He might not."

"He will," Bryce said.

Her pulse racing and the hair on the back of her neck standing up with every whine the wounded dog made, Ivy called Elias's number.

He answered on the second ring, sounding remarkably awake despite it being past midnight. "Ivy? What's wrong?"

"We have a badly injured stray dog," Ivy said as Bryce made a soothing sound to the dog in the back seat. "Joe McManus found him being attacked by a pack of coyotes near his property line about twenty minutes ago. He looks like an Australian shepherd. Pretty skinny and matted fur. Multiple bite wounds to his throat and belly, and a nasty gash on his leg. Looks like it tore open his cephalic vein. Joe applied pressure before we got there, and I've bandaged it, but he's lost a lot of blood. He needs to be seen tonight. Can I bring him to the clinic?"

"Yes," he said. "I'll meet you at the clinic in ten."

"Thank you." Relief flooded through her, and she ended the call, studying Bryce in the rear-view mirror. "How is he?"

"Not great." Bryce's voice was grim.

"Hang on, buddy," Ivy said as she stepped on the gas. "Hang on."

ELIAS WAS WAITING FOR THEM OUTSIDE THE CLINIC WITH THE stretcher. He helped Bryce and Ivy lift the injured dog onto the stretcher, and they wheeled him into the back of the clinic.

Elias had brought Bella, and Bryce crouched and put her arms around the pit bull. She buried her face in Bella's thick neck as Bella licked her hands.

"Shh, boy, it's all right," Elias said to the whimpering dog as he studied the multiple bite wounds and then his back leg. "Let's get a weight on him before we move him to the table."

Ivy helped lift the dog down to the scale, keeping one hand hovering above his prone body as Elias stared at the scale.

"Forty-five point two pounds," he said. "Help me get him onto the examining table."

They lifted him to the table, and Elias studied the bloody bandage on the dog's leg before opening the dog's mouth and pressing against his gums. "He'll need a blood transfusion before we start the surgery. I'm going to give him some pain meds. Can you prep Bella for a blood draw?"

"Don't you have to do a blood test or something?" Bryce asked as Ivy grabbed the supplies.

Elias shook his head as he injected the injured dog. "No. The first transfusion can be with any type of blood. If he needs more transfusions, the blood will need to be typed and crossmatched, but this first one will be fine."

The dog had stopped whimpering, his chest rising and falling slowly as the pain meds infused his system. Elias glanced at Bryce. "Bryce, come over here and watch the dog. Make sure he doesn't fall off the table. Ivy, bring Bella to the other table. I'll need your help drawing her blood. We'll do the blood transfusion and then get him into surgery. Can you stay and help?"

"Yes," Ivy said.

Elias spared a moment to run a hand down the stray dog's bloody and matted coat. "It'll be all right, boy."

"IVY, I CAN STAY IF YOU NEED ME TO STAY," BRYCE SAID.

Ivy shook her head before hugging her hard. "It's late... or early... I don't even know at this point. Just go home and get some sleep, okay?"

"Yeah, okay." Bryce hugged her again. "Talk to him, Ives. Tell him the truth. You won't regret it."

"I love you, Bryce," Ivy said.

Bryce smiled. "Love you too, babe."

She left the clinic, and Ivy closed and locked the door before checking the time. It was just after three, but she was still full of nervous energy. Taking a deep breath, she walked to the back of the clinic, sticking her head into the dog room.

After the surgery, they'd moved the stray dog into one of the larger kennels with heated flooring. The dog was lying in a nest of blankets, and Elias was crouched over him with a stethoscope pressed against the dog's chest.

"Good boy." Elias ran a gentle hand down the dog's side and then scratched his cheek. The dog turned its head and licked Elias' hand before sighing and resting his head on the blankets again.

"You're a good old boy," Elias said before petting him again. "Rest now."

The lump in Ivy's throat was roughly the size of Mount Rushmore. She swallowed past it with difficulty and walked quietly to Elias's office, sinking onto the small cot. She hugged her knees and smiled at Elias when he walked into the office.

"Hey."

"Hi," he said.

Bella was leaning against her legs, and she patted the dog's side. "You're such a good girl, Bella-boo. You saved that dog's life. Yes, you did, sweet girl."

The dog grinned at her happily, her tail thumping against the floor as Elias watched them quietly.

"Will you sit with me?" Ivy patted the cot mattress, her breath catching when Elias hesitated.

After a moment, he joined her, easing down beside her but making sure their thighs didn't touch. She chewed on her bottom lip. "Thank you for helping the dog tonight, Elias."

He shrugged, but she could see the anger lurking in the tenseness of his jaw. "It's my job, Ivy. Why didn't you go home with Bryce? I can keep an eye on the dog by myself."

She reached for his hand and then stopped herself. "There's something I wanted to talk to you about."

He ran his hand over the stubble on his jaw. "It's late and I'm tired. Could we do this another time?"

"It won't take long, I promise," she said.

He stared at the snow falling outside the office window. "Yeah, okay. Go ahead."

She licked her lips, listening to the quiet tick of the clock on the wall and the even sound of Elias's breathing. When he shifted on the cot next to her, she knew she had to start talking.

"When Ray first asked me out, I said no. I said no multiple times," she said. "The ironic thing is, I didn't say no because his father was the rescue's biggest donor, but because even back then," she hesitated and then blurted it out, "even back then, I knew it was you that I really wanted."

He stiffened beside her, his hands squeezing his knees compulsively. She hurried on. "It didn't seem right to date Ray when I was so attracted to you, but Ray was pretty persistent and charming, and I was lonely. I knew I didn't have a chance with you, so I told myself to go ahead and date Ray. That maybe I would start to feel the same sort of attraction I felt for you."

She studied her hands. "I never did, at least not in the way I should have. I liked Ray, and I was attracted to him, but it wasn't the same way I felt about you. Not by a long shot. When Ray started growing distant and weird only a few months after we started dating, I was actually relieved. I figured he was going to break up with me, and I was okay with that. I was deceiving him about my feelings, and I felt awful about it."

She fell silent for a few minutes. Elias glanced at her. "What happened?"

She smiled at him. "I was supposed to go to Ray's place one night, but we had a sick dog. I was looking after it, and then Bryce showed up and told me to go to Ray's. She said she would take care of the dog. She's always talking about how my work/life balance sucks."

She studied her hands again. "She's right. Anyway, I drove to Ray's, but I didn't text him beforehand. I thought it would be a fun surprise, so I picked up his favourite pizza and beer before heading over. I wanted to do something nice for him because I was feeling so guilty. You know?"

"Yeah, I get it," he said.

"I let myself into his place, and it was dark, but I could see a light on in the bedroom."

"Shit," Elias said.

"I found him in bed with Cynthia Waters. They were going at it like bunnies."

Elias took her hand, linking their fingers together, and she could have wept with relief. "I'm sorry, Ivy."

"Me too," she said. "Long story short, I broke it off with Ray. But he told me that if I told anyone I'd caught him cheating, he'd get his father to stop donating to the rescue."

"Asshole," Elias said. His hand tightened on hers. "He actually said that?"

She nodded. "He did." I was terrified he would do it, so I didn't say a word. He smeared my name to anyone who would listen. Told everyone I was cruel and heartless, and dumped him because I couldn't love him the way he loved me."

"Fucking asshole," Elias said.

"I never told anyone but Bryce and Nana the real truth, but it didn't matter. Ray's dad stopped donating to the rescue because he was so angry that I had broken his boy's heart. That was last January, and the rescue has been struggling ever since. If you hadn't offered to write off the rescue's vet bill, we probably would have closed by the end of this month."

He turned to face her, cupping her face and resting his forehead against hers. "I'm sorry, Ivy. I'm sorry for what I said to you, for how I treated you and -"

"No." She gripped the back of his neck and pressed a brief

kiss against his mouth. "I'm sorry, Elias. What I said about you not helping the rescue was gross and unfair. In my heart, I knew you would never do that. I know you're a good and kind man – you're the best man I know – but I'd just had a nasty conversation with Ray's dad in the grocery store, and I was feeling awful and I … well, I panicked."

"Understandable," he said.

"It isn't," she replied. "You didn't deserve to be treated that way, and I am truly sorry. Can you forgive me for what I said?"

"Yes."

Relief flooded through her, making her slump a little. "Just like that?"

"Just like that," he said. "It's easy to forgive the person you love."

She straightened and stared at him before reaching out with trembling fingers to trace his jaw. "You love me?"

"Yes," he said. "I love you, Ivy West."

She could feel the smile stretching her cheeks wide. "I love you too, Elias Hart."

"Good," he said before pulling her into his lap and kissing her hard on the mouth. "Because I am crazily, stupidly, ridiculously in love with you, and I can't imagine my life without you."

She threaded her fingers through his thick, dark hair. "You're the best thing that's ever happened to me, Elias."

"Does that mean," he reached into his pocket and pulled out his grandmother's ring, "that you'll wear this again?"

"Have you been carrying that around all week?" she said.

"Maybe," he replied.

She laughed. "You really want to be engaged? We don't know that much about each other."

He shrugged. "So, we have a long engagement and you

can really get to know me before you're stuck with me for the rest of your life."

"I wouldn't exactly call it stuck," she said as he slipped the ring onto her finger. She admired the small diamond. "I love this ring."

"I can buy you a different one," he said.

"Don't you dare. This one is perfect," she replied before kissing him again. "Now, Dr. Hart, show me how much you love me."

"With pleasure, Ms. West."

"How's he doing?" Elias asked as Ivy closed the kennel door.

"Good. He ate well and had a pee this morning," Ivy said. She petted the dog's soft ears through the kennel before following Elias back into his office.

He rubbed the back of his neck and yawned. "God, I'm tired."

"Lie down on the cot and have a nap," Ivy said. "I'll keep an eye on the dog."

He shook his head. "Nah, I'm good. Besides, he'll be okay on his own for a few hours. He's had his morning dose of pain meds, and they'll keep him a bit sedated. It's just after nine. Why don't we grab a quick breakfast and head back to my place for a nap? I'll come back to check on him and give him his antibiotics and pain meds this afternoon."

She leaned against him, resting her cheek on his chest. "That sounds like a great idea. I'd love – oh, hold on."

She pulled her phone from her pocket and answered it. "Hi, Nana. Yep, the dog made it through the night. He's doing well, all things considered. Elias and I are going to grab a bite to eat before heading back to his place for a nap."

She paused before smiling. "Yes, I did. Thank you. I'm happy for us too."

Elias kissed the back of her neck, sliding his arms around her waist and holding her tight as she listened to her grandmother speak. Her slender body stiffened, and she said, "Wait, he did what? Are you serious? Right now? He came by right now?"

He rubbed her hip, trying to ease the tension in her body. She slumped against him. "I can't – I can't believe it. Nana, that's... I mean, do you know what this means? Holy shit! This is a friggin' miracle! Yeah, okay, I'm gonna go too. I love you, and I'll talk to you later this afternoon."

She ended the call and swivelled in his arms, her small body vibrating with excitement and her eyes bright. A piece of her blonde hair was stuck to her cheek, and he smoothed it back. "What's going on?"

"You're not going to believe this."

"What?" he asked.

"Mr. Dorchester – Ray's father – he just dropped by the house. He gave Nana a cheque for the rescue, and he said he'd be continuing with his yearly donations again."

"Seriously?"

"Yes!" She threw her arms around his waist. "When I talked to him at the grocery store, he made me pretty angry, and I finally told him that Ray had cheated on me. I didn't expect him to care about it, but I guess he did."

"That's wonderful," he said.

"You haven't heard the best part," she said. "The cheque he gave Nana wasn't just a yearly donation for this year. He also added the donation he would have given last year. Do you know how many animals we can help now?"

She kissed him hard on the mouth, and he picked her up and swung her in a circle until she laughed and pounded on his back. He set her on her feet and pressed another kiss against her mouth. "I'm so happy for you."

"I'm happy for the animals we can save," she said.

He studied her flushed and happy face before smiling at her. "I love you, Ivy West."

Her smile widened, and she touched his face with gentle fingers. "I love you too, Elias Hart."

Keep reading for an excerpt from Elizabeth Kelly's FREE small town romance,
"Sweet Harmony".

SWEET HARMONY EXCERPT

When the doorbell rang, Kira smoothed down her blonde hair and checked her reflection in the toaster. Not that it mattered what she looked like. This wasn't a first date, for God's sake.

She headed out of the kitchen and down the hallway. Two long windows flanked the front door, and she could see one tanned arm and hand through the right one. Her dentist had big hands.

You know what they say about big hands.

She flushed and tossed that errant thought out of her head before opening the door. She smiled at the dark-haired man standing on her front porch.

"Hello, Dr. MacMillan."

"Hello, Ms. Walker," he said.

There was a moment of awkward silence, and then she stepped back. "Call me Kira. Please, come in."

He stepped into the house, and she shut the door before squeezing past him. "Would you like something to drink? I have water, iced tea and soda. Or I can make coffee."

"An iced tea would be fine," he said.

As he followed her toward the kitchen, she wondered if he was checking out her ass in her yoga pants. She knew she didn't have a great body. She was on the thin side, and she secretly coveted Grace's full curves. She scoffed inwardly. Who was she kidding? Forget Grace's curves, she'd take Addison's very respectable C-cup boobs if given the chance. She was barely a B-cup, and her cleavage was thanks to the miracle invention of the century – the push-up bra.

Why she even thought her dentist would check out her ass was ridiculous. It was flat and –

Hey, Kira? Maybe you should stop thinking about your own damn tits and ass and get the man his iced tea.

Dr. MacMillan was hovering in the kitchen doorway while she stood blankly next to the fridge, and she gave him an embarrassed smile. "Sorry. Have a seat, and I'll get that iced tea."

"Thank you," he said.

She poured each of them a glass of iced tea and perched on the edge of the chair across from him. He drank some iced tea before saying, "It's good. Thanks."

"I like it a little on the sweet side," she said. "My brother says it's way too sweet and that I'll rot my teeth right out of my head, but I guess that's why I go to see you, right? To keep my teeth from rotting out of my head when I eat too much sweet stuff?"

Kira! Enough!

She shut her mouth with a snap. Fuck, what was wrong with her? Why was she so damn nervous? Sure, Dr. MacMillan was handsome enough, but he wasn't Daniel. She closed her eyes for a moment and conjured up an image of Daniel. It calmed her a little, and she took a deep breath. Daniel's blond hair and dark blue eyes were what she wanted.

Dr. MacMillan's eyes might be blue, but they were so light they were almost transparent. She could see none of the warmth and humour in them that Daniel's gaze had. In fact, her dentist was currently staring at her like she was some new and interesting species of bug he had discovered crawling up his leg.

She cleared her throat. "Sorry, I babble when I'm nervous."

He took another drink of iced tea. "You have a nice home."

"Thank you. It was my childhood home. It belongs to my brother now, but he didn't want to live here. My parents died a few years ago, and being in the house brought on too many sad memories for him. I love living here, though. It makes me feel closer to my mom and dad, you know?"

She closed her mouth again. Holy shit, she was making the worst first impression ever.

"I'm sorry about your parents." His voice was a low rasp, and the sound of it sent the weirdest shiver down her spine.

"Thank you," she replied. "So, um, Grace said we could help each other with our problems."

He nodded. "Possibly."

She waited, trying not to sigh in frustration, when he said nothing else. His silence was beginning to unnerve her. Daniel was chatty and always the life of the party. She could barely get a word in edgewise when she was with him, and she loved that. She loved his bold brashness and how he lit up a room when he walked into it.

Her dentist hardly made an impact. Hell, she'd met him how many times in his office, and she had no impression of him at all. He was just a masked guy who came in and checked her teeth at the end of the cleaning.

"So, you need a date for your cousin's wedding?" she asked.

"Yes," he said, "and you need a boyfriend to make Daniel Moore jealous."

His voice had the slightest hint of derision, and she immediately blushed. It was evident that he thought she was an idiot.

"You know what? Never mind, Dr. MacMillan." She stood and dumped her iced tea down the sink. "This isn't going to work. I'll show you out now."

She stalked toward the front door. She could hear him behind her, but before she could open the door, he wrapped his long fingers around her wrist. The touch of his skin against hers made another one of those little shivers zip down her spinal cord. She froze and turned to stare up at him.

"I'm sorry," he said. "I'm being an ass."

"Yes, you are."

He sighed and dropped her wrist before raking his hand through his dark hair. "I apologize. Also, if we're going to fake date, you should call me Connor."

"Why are you even here, Connor?" she asked. "It's obvious you think this is a stupid idea."

"It isn't," he said. "I'm just -"

He paused and rubbed at one temple. "What if this doesn't work?"

"What do you mean?"

"What if our fake dating doesn't make Daniel jealous? Will you still go with me to my cousin's wedding? Still pretend to be my girlfriend?"

"Yes," she said.

"What if it does work? Then what? You start dating Daniel, and I'm headed to Willington alone."

"Well, your cousin's wedding is in a month, right?"

"Yes."

"We don't have to start fake dating right away. We can give it a couple of weeks and use that time to learn more about each other. It's probably a good idea if we know more than each other's names. It'll be more believable if we know personal stuff about each other. That leaves only two weeks until your cousin's wedding. I think it'll take more than a couple of weeks to make Daniel jealous," she said.

"Do I have your word that you'll attend the wedding with me?" he asked.

"Yes," she said. "I'll be there, no matter what."

"Then we have an agreement," Connor said. "You'll pose as my girlfriend at my cousin's wedding, and I'll help you make Daniel seethe with jealousy and realize that you're his soul mate."

She gave him a dirty look. "You don't have to make it sound so juvenile."

He just shrugged, and she reached for the front door. "Thank you. I'll get your number from Grace and text you in the next few days about meeting to go over personal stuff."

"There's just one more thing," Connor said.

"What?"

"This." He gripped the back of her neck and pulled her forward. She made a decidedly stupid-sounding squeak when he bent his dark head and pressed his mouth against hers. She stood stock-still with her eyes wide and unblinking as he slid his other arm around her waist and pulled her against his hard body.

When he sucked on her lower lip, a strange tingle went through her lower body, and another small sound escaped her lips. This one, embarrassingly enough, sounded like a moan, and she tried to step back. His hand tightened around her neck, holding her completely immobile. When his tongue slid across her upper lip, she heard another of those odd moan-like noises as her eyes drifted shut.

God, he smells so good, she thought bewilderedly as he tilted her head back. He kissed her again, his lips warm and weirdly persuasive, and it took her a minute to realize she was returning his kiss.

Kira! Stop kissing your dentist!

It was solid advice, but her body was completely and blissfully betraying her. She pressed up against Connor and put her arms around his neck. He was so tall that it was a real stretch to do it, but she liked the way it forced her breasts against his chest.

His tongue licked the seam of her mouth. Her head whirling and her pussy suddenly throbbing, she parted her lips. He slid his tongue between them and tasted her with slow, long licks that made Kira shudder with pleasure. He tasted sweet, like the iced tea he had been drinking. When she pushed her tongue into his mouth with a decided lack of finesse, he slid his fingers into her hair and tugged her back.

"Slow," he whispered.

She blushed fiercely. For roughly a nanosecond, she thought about telling him to stop, but then his warm mouth returned to hers, and he was urging her tongue back into his mouth with slow licks of his. She slowed down and mimicked the slow strokes of his tongue.

He groaned quietly. Besides his low whisper, it was the first sound he had made since kissing her. It flamed the lust in her belly even higher. She had a feeling that the icy Dr. Connor MacMillan never lost control. The idea that kissing her could make that control slip, even a little, was deliciously intoxicating.

She arched her back and rubbed her abdomen against the

hardness pressing into it. Connor was hard. He was hard for her, and that sent another flickering flame of excitement through her nerve endings. She rubbed her small breasts against him and wondered what she could do to get him to touch them. Her nipples were almost painfully hard and poking against her bra. A sudden vision of Connor sucking on them brought on a gush of liquid that soaked the crotch of her panties.

He pulled away abruptly, and she would have fallen in a boneless heap to the floor if he hadn't steadied her. She stared dumbly at him before reaching up and touching her trembling, swollen lips.

"Why-why did you do that?" she whispered.

"If we're posing as boyfriend and girlfriend, it's going to require physical touching and kissing," he said.

She felt like she'd been through the wringer, but he wasn't even out of breath. If it hadn't been for the way his dick still strained at the front of his pants, she would have thought he was completely unaffected by the kiss between them.

"O-only when we're around other people." She couldn't seem to stop stuttering or touching her swollen mouth.

He gave her an impatient look. "It won't look very realistic if we kiss each other like it's the first time we've ever kissed. And I wanted to see if we had chemistry."

"Do we?" she asked like an idiot.

A brief smile crossed his face, sending a weird tingle down the base of her spine. "Yes. I think so, anyway."

She didn't reply, and he patted her shoulder like she was his sister. "That's a good thing, Kira. It will make it appear more real."

"Uh, right," she said.

He studied her. "How many men have you kissed before?"

"Why?"

"You're not," he paused, "great at kissing."

Her face was so red she was nearly sweating, and she gave him a furious look. "That's a really rude thing to say."

"No, just honest. We'll need to practice some more."

She wanted to tell him to take his idea of practice kissing and stuff it up his piehole, but strangely, the thought of kissing him again wasn't entirely unpleasant. Besides, as much as it was a blow to her ego, he probably had a point. She'd kissed two men before him, and neither of them had provoked the type of reaction that her dentist's kiss did.

He opened the front door and asked, "What time do you work tomorrow?"

"Uh, I need to be at the office by nine."

"I'll stop by at eight, and we'll practice." He left, shutting the door quietly behind him, and she sank against the wall, her fingers still tracing her lower lip. What the hell just happened?

ABOUT THE AUTHOR

Elizabeth Kelly was born and raised in Ontario, Canada. She moved west as a teenager and now lives in Alberta with her husband and a menagerie of pets. She firmly believes that a person can survive solely on sushi and coffee, and only her husband's mad cooking skills prevents her from proving that theory.

For more information about Elizabeth, check out her website at

www.elizabethkelly.ca

- facebook.com/EKellyBooks
- instagram.com/elizabethkelly_author
- amazon.com/Elizabeth-Kelly/e/B00EOHZ0MS
- bookbub.com/authors/elizabeth-kelly
- bsky.app/profile/elizabethkelly.bsky.social
- threads.net/@elizabethkelly_author

ALSO BY ELIZABETH KELLY

Tempted Series

Tempted

Twice Tempted

Forever Tempted

Breathless

Tempted Trilogy (Books 1-3)

Red Moon Series

Red Moon

Red Moon Rising

Dark Moon

Alpha Moon

Pale Moon

The Recruit Series

The Recruit (Book One)

The Recruit (Book Two)

The Recruit (Book Three)

The Recruit (Book Four)

The Recruit (Book Five)

The Recruit (Book Six)

The Shifters Series

Willow and the Wolf (Book One)

Ava and the Bear (Book Two)

Katarina and the Bird (Book Three)

Porter's Mate (Book Four)

Bria and the Tiger (Book Five)

Rosalie Undone (Book Six)

The Dragon's Mate (Book Seven)

Rise of the Jaguar (Book Eight)

The Assassin and the Bear (Book Nine)

Elora and the Crow (Book Ten)

The Draax Series

Reign (Book One)

Rule (Book Two)

Rebel (Book Three)

Surrender (Book Four)

Survive (Book Five)

Salvation (Book Six)

Harmony Falls Series

Sweet Harmony (Book One)

Perfect Harmony (Book Two)

Forbidden Harmony (Book Three)

Redeeming Harmony (Book Four)

Absolute Harmony (Novella)

Beautiful Harmony (Book Five)

Reckless Harmony (Book Six)

Seasoned Romance Series

Bet Your Heart on Me (Book One)

Take a Chance on Me (Book Two)

Place Your Trust in Me (Book Three)

Individual Books

The Necessary Engagement

Amelia's Touch

The Rancher's Daughter

Healing Gabriel

The Contract

A Home for Lily

Saving Charlotte

Shameless

The Fairy Tales Collection

Broken

Always

An Unlikely Seduction

Holiday Romance

The Christmas Wife

The Christmas Rescue

The Christmas Nanny

The Christmas Boss

Sordid Games